"Why are you he

"I don't suppose you'll accept saving you from an intruder as an answer," Doug replied.

"Not likely, since I had it handled." Sort of.

As nice as it would be to believe that, he couldn't have known she'd needed saving at that very moment. She had to stay upright. If not, Doug would probably throw her over his shoulder and take her to whoever he reported to for that questioning he'd threatened her with.

Was he friend or foe? He acted as if he cared. But then at times he was like a runaway train. Nothing would stop him from getting what he wanted.

He broke into her thoughts. "Thinking about running again?"

"I was—" Her voice gave out. Sabine touched her throat. It was tender from the intruder's grip. She sucked in a deep breath. It was all she could do.

"Sabine." His voice sounded far away, like he was speaking underwater.

The floor swept up toward her and Sabine descended into darkness....

LISA PHILLIPS

A British expat who grew up an hour outside of London, Lisa attended Calvary Chapel Bible College. There she met her husband who's from California, but nobody's perfect. It wasn't until her Bible College graduation that she figured out she was a writer (someone told her). Since then she's taken the Apprentice and Journeyman writing courses with the Christian Writers Guild, and discovered a penchant for high-stakes stories of mayhem and disaster where you can find made-for-each-other love that always ends in happily ever after.

Lisa can be found in Idaho wearing either flip-flops or cowgirl boots, depending on the season. She leads worship with her husband at their local church. Together they have two children, a sparkly Little Princess and a Mini Daddy, and two bunny rabbits.

You can tweet Lisa (@lisaphillipsbks) or to find out more visit www.authorlisaphillips.com.

DOUBLE AGENT

LISA PHILLIPS

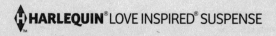
HARLEQUIN® LOVE INSPIRED® SUSPENSE

Recycling programs
for this product may
not exist in your area.

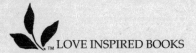

LOVE INSPIRED BOOKS

ISBN-13: 978-0-373-44598-1

DOUBLE AGENT

Copyright © 2014 by Lisa Phillips

www.Harlequin.com

Printed in U.S.A.

But now in Christ Jesus you who once were far off
have been brought near by the blood of Christ.
—*Ephesians* 2:13

For my sister Beverley,
who read all fifty-seven thousand versions of
my Speed Date pitch before declaring it was FINE.

I guess it was.

ONE

"What is she doing here?" Army Sergeant Major Doug Richardson hissed out a breath as three guys crowded around him in the commandeered apartment, his Delta Force teammates.

Doug put his eye back to the viewfinder. The glass-fronted bistro across the street was next door to a swanky hotel. The eatery was the current location of their target, who sat at the crowded restaurant bar with his aviator sunglasses on like some kind of hotshot movie star. Doug felt his teammates gather around him—Barker, Hanning and Perkins. The fifth member, Franklin, was positioned in the hotel lobby.

Doug had to be mistaken. Was it really her? Surely there were other women in the world with that stride, with the same dark—almost black—hair that caught the light like that?

But there she was.

She glanced around the restaurant like she was looking for an empty seat. Of course the only one available was the stool beside the target. She had no idea who this guy was. Or that this was a golden opportunity for his team to observe Christophe Parelli conducting business. And there she was, right in the middle of it.

The woman he'd met a handful of times was quiet and well-spoken—not the type to smile like that at the man who had financed her brother's murder.

Their team had hoped Parelli would meet with the person he worked for. In an ideal world, the guy would be here to meet the person known only as the Raven.

Years of team effort would pull together in a result that brought them the mysterious head of the crime syndicate they'd been chasing for what seemed like forever. The idea that Sabine might be Parelli's contact was insane. Doug wasn't even going to entertain the idea that she might be the Raven, because that meant everything he felt was wrong.

At the funeral she'd stood alone beside her brother's grave while the wind had whipped her hair around her face. The weight of her grief had about killed Doug. He'd almost missed the strain when she was handed the folded-up flag, but it had been there. If anyone touched her, it would have broken the tight hold she had on her emotions.

That was two weeks ago now, and Doug hadn't been able to get her out of his head since. Though he'd had an instinct that this mission was going to go wrong, the last thing he thought it might be was her. She was supposed to be at home, grieving the loss of her brother.

Not in the middle of the operation to bring down the man who killed him.

Doug growled, then simply said, "Sabine."

Sabine Laduca settled herself on the stool and signaled the bartender. Her stomach churned, but she pasted on a smile. "Diet soda, please."

She smoothed down the skirt of her dress and walked her mind through her training. Her whole adult life had prepared her for this moment, and she could not screw it up. Years of instruction with the CIA, coupled with years of missions that took her all over the world and tested her beyond her skills… It all came down to now.

The man beside her was handsome enough, she supposed, if you went for the overly styled Mediterranean-playboy type. That wasn't Sabine's thing. Her type ran more toward a gorgeous Delta Force team leader with almond-colored skin.

The man who seemed to always be on her mind was the perfect mix of a tall African-American army general and a beautiful Caucasian woman. She'd seen a picture of his parents only once and didn't know too much about them, but it was easy to tell he'd been given the best features from both.

Unlike her.

Sabine shifted in her seat and shot the target a cordial smile, like she was perfectly content with her own thoughts.

It really was too bad that life threw a wrench in every single plan she made. Not so much disrupting her dreams, but more like completely obliterating them. Just not this plan—please—because this mission was more important than anything she'd ever done.

Contact with the target wasn't sanctioned, but she needed Parelli's fingerprint to gain access to his hotel room. There were other ways she could have gotten it, but there was no way she was going to pass this up.

This was her chance to look in the eyes of the man who had financed her brother's murder.

Despite being a fully trained agent for years, she'd never killed anyone. It almost seemed fitting for this man to be her first. Except that revenge would be way too easy. Sabine wasn't after quick and painless; her broken heart cried out for the complete destruction of everything this man held dear—which for this guy was money and nothing else.

Retrieving the hard drive from his computer was only the first step of the plan. Her handler's instructions were clear: no bloodshed and no emotions—just get the computer data and get out. The tech guys he passed the hard drive to would do the rest of the work.

She glanced at the target and realized he'd pulled his sunglasses down his nose with one finger and was taking her in. Sabine pursed her mouth and put on her best British accent. "Lovely weather we're having, isn't it?"

He flashed his bleached teeth. "This is the Caribbean. Unless it's hurricane season, it's always lovely weather."

She laughed, trying her best to sound charmed. Her phone rang, stalling what she'd been about to say. It took everything in her to hold back her surprise at the number on screen, but she smiled as though delighted.

"Hello?" How long would it take him to ask why she'd put on a British accent?

"What do you think you are doing?"

She blinked. That was all the reaction she allowed to the fact that he'd roared. "Is everything okay, darling?"

"No, everything is not okay. Get up and leave the restaurant. Now."

He knew where she was. Sabine transferred the phone to her other ear. Hopefully the target hadn't heard Doug shout. She wasn't about to let the Delta Force soldier interfere in her CIA-sanctioned mission. Too bad he was still yelling, which meant she couldn't get a word in. Didn't the army know that an operative was going to be here?

"You have no idea what you're in the middle of."

And he had no idea that she wasn't a banker, but a spy.

Busted. Or did Doug think she was chasing her brother's killer on her own? Either way, he needed to get off the phone. "Of course, darling, that sounds like a splendid idea. I'll meet you there once I've finished at the shops."

"No delays, Sabine. This better not be what I think it is."

The bartender removed the target's drink and replaced it with a fresh one.

"I go where I want, when I want. As I said, I'll be there when I've finished." She hung up.

"Boyfriend?"

"He wishes." She held out her hand to the target. "I'm Sabine."

He kissed her knuckles. "Christophe Parelli."

Like his name was supposed to mean something to her? Well, it meant something, all right, and none of what she knew was good. It meant the son of a weapons dealer being groomed to take over Daddy's business. It meant too much money and too little sense. In general, trouble with a capital *T.*

"It's a pleasure to meet you, but I must dash. The day is waning, and there's still plenty of his money to spend."

Across the restaurant she looked back over her shoulder to smile and wave, but his attention was already elsewhere. She skirted the edge of the bar, swiped his empty glass from the tray and strode in the direction of the restrooms. With the glass tucked away in the mammoth purse she'd bought online because it went with her dress, Sabine went down the hall past the ladies' room all the way to the exit door at the end.

Five minutes later Sabine placed the image of Christophe Parelli's fingerprint on the hotel room's door scanner and covered it with the base of her thumb. The reader needed body heat, but she didn't want to confuse it with two overlapping prints. The light on the scanner switched to green, and the lock clicked open.

Doug's team was probably here on the same mission. Too bad for them that she was going to get to Parelli's computer first. She'd always had a problem with sharing.

Her steps were muffled on the plush carpet. Despite the price tag that came with this suite, it was still just a hotel room. Something inside her yearned for home, but she pushed it away. Now wasn't the time for that.

The desktop was bare. The safe in the bedroom closet was shut and locked. Sabine entered the code she'd memorized and held her breath.

She drew out the laptop, flipped it over and pulled a screwdriver from her purse. The hard drive slid out into her hand. She secured the cover again, set the laptop back in the safe and glanced at the watch face on her bracelet.

Still enough time to search the room.

Clothes were strewn over every available surface, and the bathroom counter was cluttered with men's hair-care products. Sabine rolled her eyes. It wasn't like he was a movie star or a male model or anything like that.

Satisfied there was nothing else worth taking, she turned to exit the suite.

The lock on the outer door clicked.

Her breath stuttered and a blue baseball cap appeared between the now open door and the frame. She shoved the hard drive in her purse and blanked her face.

Doug's gaze found her in the middle of the bedroom— dark caramel eyes that gave nothing away. He filled the doorway, so tall that, if he didn't shave his head, his hair could have touched the frame. So wide it was a wonder he didn't get stuck. Sabine was tall herself, but Doug made her feel small in a way that had nothing to do with self-worth and everything to do with comfort.

Her brother had been skinny and baby faced his whole life—even at thirty-one years old, Ben had looked more like a kid playing dress-up in his uniform than an actual soldier. Doug, on the other hand, made that dark green dress uniform look good. Mouthwateringly good.

Today his navy blue T-shirt was damp with the heat of the day, and his cargo shorts and ball cap were every tourist's go-to apparel. Only there was nothing about him that blended in.

Doug closed the door and held up the clear plastic with Christophe's fingerprint on it. She shut her eyes. She'd left it on the scanner. She wanted to reprimand herself over such a simple mistake, but put a hand on her hip instead. "What are you doing here?" Her voice shook more than she'd have liked, but it was too late now.

"What am I— Seriously? That's what you're going with?" He glanced around the room. "Let me guess… CIA?"

She stiffened. He wasn't supposed to get it right the first time.

"Did Ben know about this?"

Her stomach surged like a storm-fueled wave. "You don't get to talk about my brother."

He stepped closer. "This is about him, right? Ben is the reason why we're all after Parelli."

She hated that he pitied her. And that his voice had to go soft. He'd been there when Ben was murdered by a sniper on what was supposed to be a routine mission. As far as she was concerned, that meant Doug was responsible.

"We need to talk but not here. Let's go."

Sabine blinked. "Excuse me? I happen to be working."

Doug looked away. "Copy that, California." He surged forward. "Someone's coming. We have to hide."

Apparently "California" was the handle of the newest

member of Doug's team—the electronics expert who had replaced her brother, Ben. She didn't want that thought to touch her, but the knife slipped in, anyway.

She loved Ben's old team: Barker, the big African-American Texan who always smiled; Hanning, who looked like a male model in his designer clothes; Franklin, so ordinary in appearance that she had almost overlooked him, until she got to know him and found out his heart was large.

Doug dragged her to the closet and closed the partition door so they were shrouded in darkness. He pulled on her arm and tried to get her to move deeper into the closet, but she shrugged him off.

"Sabine," he hissed.

Nose to the wood, she studied the suite through the slim gap in the door. "They're here."

Christophe Parelli sauntered in and tossed his sunglasses on the bed. A woman followed him, wearing a red dress similar to Sabine's. She, too, had long, dark hair. In fact, the resemblance was so striking that Sabine sucked in a breath through her nose.

The woman moved to the fridge in the corner and pulled out a glass bottle of amber liquid. She took her time pouring two drinks and then handed one to Christophe. With the limited view Sabine had, she couldn't make out the woman's features. Her bearing was familiar, but Sabine couldn't place where she'd seen her before.

Doug touched Sabine's shoulder. She took another deep breath and expelled it, low and slow. As soon as the woman and Parelli left, then Doug and Sabine would be able to get out of there.

Christophe held up his glass. "A toast, to a beautiful relationship."

"Yes." The woman took a sip of her drink, while she

watched Christophe swallow his. "Too bad it cannot continue."

Christophe jerked. The glass fell. It hit the carpet with a dull thud. His hand grasped his throat. "What did you do?" His voice was raspy.

Though the woman laughed, there was no humor in the sound. "You didn't think I could let you live, did you? So naive. You, my dear, are a liability, and liabilities must be eradicated."

"But—"

Christophe dropped to his knees, wheezing. Doug pulled on her arm as he tried again to draw her away from the horrific scene, but she held fast. Something about the woman would help identify her. Anything was better than admitting Sabine was seeing someone take their last breath. Again.

Doug's hand slid from her elbow, and he stilled her fingers with his.

The woman sighed. "I know it pains you to hear it. But you are one small part, an insignificant part that I cannot allow to remain free. So goodbye, my dear. It really was a pleasure."

Christophe collapsed to the floor. Sabine could barely see his chest move. The woman strode from the room, leaving the door wide open.

"She's gone."

Doug opened the closet door. "Copy that, California. Ten minutes."

Sabine forced her gaze away from the dead man. "What?"

"Rendezvous. Let's go."

She didn't move. The woman who had killed Christophe had probably used some kind of fast-acting poison that closed the airways and stopped the heart. Easy enough to get, and who cared if it showed up in an autopsy? The guy wasn't any less dead.

Her red dress had been too much like Sabine's. And that wasn't the only similarity. There was only one logical conclusion.

"I killed him."

TWO

"That woman. She was... It was supposed to look like I did it. Multiple people saw Christophe and me talking at the bar in that restaurant. People would have seen that woman come up here with him. We have the same build. The same long, dark hair. The same red dress." Sabine blinked. "Who knew I'd be here?"

Understanding washed over his features. "We still have to go. More so if you're going to be the number one suspect."

Her breath came faster and faster, and she pressed her fists to the sides of her face. She was going to be framed for this. Sabine stumbled back; her ankle rolled. She hit the floor and cried out.

Doug hauled her to her feet. "We have to go."

"Please." She didn't know what she was asking for.

"You want to stay here with the dead guy?" He half held, half carried her down the hall. "We need to get gone."

Her brain spun until she was hardly able to string two thoughts together. She saw her handler, Neil, at the park under a Saturday-morning sun briefing her on the mission. "She made it look like I killed him."

Doug glanced at her, still pulling her along. "Sabine." His voice was a warning.

She forced away the pain in her ankle to keep up with him. Behind them there was a shout, followed by the rush of feet. Sabine looked back as two men in suits broke into a run.

"Time to go," Doug said.

They sprinted for the exit. Adrenaline pulsed through her. It cleared her mind. Sabine found her own steam and pulled away from him. Doug grabbed her hand again as they closed the distance to the stairwell; he punched open the door and pulled her up instead of down.

"What are you doing? We should go to the lobby. The exit."

He didn't slow, just took each flight of stairs at a punishing pace. Every step shot fire from her twisted ankle up her leg.

"Less talking. More running."

A door slammed below. Dress shoes pounded up the stairwell. The echo bounced off the walls.

"We should split up," she said.

Doug's hand tightened on hers. They rounded the landing on the next floor and continued up. "California, get us out of here."

Sweat ran down her back. Sabine pushed through the strain in her muscles and concentrated on each step. Behind them the two goons raced up the stairs.

"Copy that." Doug yanked her arm and changed direction. Sabine hissed with the pain and trailed him through a door into a hallway where rooms stretched out before them on either side. Doug jerked her again, opened a door that said Maintenance and swept her inside.

The door clicked closed, and they were enveloped in darkness yet again. All she could hear was heavy breathing, though Doug didn't seem to be nearly as winded as she was. It was barely a second before the stairwell door opened.

"Where'd they go?" The voice spoke in Italian.

Sabine held her breath. Christophe was Italian. These were probably the bodyguards Daddy had assigned to him.

A different voice replied, also in Italian. "You search this floor. I'll take the stairs again. Call me if you find them."

The two men dispersed.

Sabine exhaled. "Let's get out of here."

Doug held up one finger, but Sabine wasn't in the mood to be told what to do. He must have seen it on her face because, before she could move, he was between her and the door.

He moved his face an inch from hers and kept his voice low. "Now isn't the time for showmanship."

Everything she'd just seen through the crack in the closet door came back in a rush. The woman had put something in Christophe's drink that made him fall to the floor.

"If this gets out, it'll end my career," she whispered.

Doug shifted. "Quiet."

Where was the Doug who'd been in the hotel room, the one who looked at her with kindness and compassion? Where was the man who had stood by her at her brother's graveside? This guy was the army Special Ops soldier with the permanent callus between his thumb and index finger on his gun hand. Mr. Team Leader was clearly used to giving orders that were obeyed without question.

Sabine had never been good at being told what to do. "So this is your big escape plan, huh? Hiding in a closet?"

He didn't say anything. He didn't need to. In the darkness of the tiny room, frustration came off him in waves. "Copy that, California."

Doug eased the door open and glanced both ways. Sabine took a step to follow. Her ankle gave out and she collapsed, biting back what she really wanted to say. Her right ankle was swollen around the straps of her shoe.

Doug crouched and unbuckled both of them. He lifted her swollen foot and winced. "You need a bandage. Probably some crutches."

She couldn't let herself get distracted by the kindness in his voice. It was normally deep, almost melodic in tone, and she liked listening to him shout instructions when the guys played their extremely intense version of touch football. Now she knew that when he spoke softly in that low voice, it chased away the shivers.

"What I need is to get off the floor."

His mouth thinned, but he helped her up.

Sabine swung her purse on her shoulder and cleared the door so he could close it. "What floor is this?"

"Twelve."

No way was she going to hobble down multiple flights of stairs. She turned and limped for the elevator, not caring if he followed or not. Honest. "My room is only two floors down. I can see myself there. Thanks for your help."

"I don't think so." He kept pace with her, glancing around. "Copy that, California." He zeroed in on Sabine. "Perkins says you don't have a room."

She smirked. "Amateurs."

"Excuse me?"

They reached the elevators. When Doug didn't press the button, Sabine reached for it herself. "I bet he checked for me under my real name."

"You have another one that we don't know about?"

She smiled. "The things you don't know about me could fill the whole internet."

He folded his arms. "Evidently. For starters, how a professional…whatever you are…manages to be surprised when someone assassinates a target. I thought you guys were all about offing the bad guy."

The whole thing hit way too close to home. Seeing someone killed, despite the difference in circumstances. Well, it didn't matter. Witnessing someone's last breath wasn't something she could forget.

Sabine drew on the only thing she had left: bravado. "Do they teach stereotyping to all army soldiers, or is that just your thing?"

She stepped into the empty elevator and winced at the pain in her foot. That was the only reason she had tears in her eyes. The disappointment on Doug's face didn't have anything to do with it. Who cared what he thought of her, anyway?

"I'm sorry."

She whipped around. "Don't."

"Sabine—"

The elevator doors opened, and they both stayed silent while he walked her to her room. When the door didn't close behind her, she whirled as fast as her ankle would let her. Doug stood there, scanning the room she'd reserved. Of course he'd waltzed in right behind her. Probably thought he was going to personally escort her all the way home.

She looked around at the budget accommodations. It was a far cry from Christophe's suite, but she didn't care what it looked like. This was the room that brought her within reach of the man who was the money behind Ben's death—the man who likely knew who was responsible.

She had to know who'd fired the rifle from that rooftop. She had to know why Ben was gone. Otherwise, what was the point? But how could she find out what had happened when the biggest lead was dead? Not to mention that her retribution plan was now pointless.

She wanted to pray there was something on the hard drive that would point to who had killed Ben, but her emotions were too messed up to deal with the issue of faith just then.

There had to be evidence on there they could use, otherwise all of her investigation into classified government files, running down leads, the days of work she'd put in—everything leading up to this mission—would have been for nothing. And Sabine would be left with only the empty feeling of not being able to make sense of anything.

Doug closed the door with him on the wrong side of it. "We shouldn't stay here too long. Christophe's bodyguards might get lucky and figure out where you're staying."

"The two guys who chased us? Please. I've seen smarter sponges."

Sabine dug through her suitcase for her first-aid kit. She located an elastic bandage, sat on the edge of the bed and started to wrap her ankle. Sharp pain sliced through her foot, and she ducked her head to blow out a breath through pursed lips.

Masculine fingers covered hers. The distinction between his almond-colored skin and her olive-toned flesh made it all the more clear to her that they had little common ground. The loving family he came from was worlds away from her dingy two-bedroom childhood home where everything had gone wrong.

"Let me."

She looked up. The warmth of his fingers on hers registered, along with the look in his eye. Her throat thickened, and she forced herself to nod.

While he made quick work of the bandage, Sabine felt her heart stretch and come awake for the first time. That had never happened any of the other times she'd met

Doug—*MacArthur,* as the guys called him. The simple name suited his steady and uncomplicated nature.

At the few backyard barbecues for the team and their families that she'd attended, Sabine had always felt like an outsider. She'd been attracted to Doug, but any time they had talked he steered the conversation through small talk and never lingered for long.

He clearly didn't feel anything special for her. That was when she began to make excuses to her brother and say she had to work—which wasn't a lie. Now that Ben was dead, she wished she hadn't made him look at her that way or feel sorry for her.

Sabine cleared her throat. "So why are you guys here?"

"Why don't you tell me why you're here first?"

"You tell me, and I'll tell you. Otherwise I have nothing to say." It was juvenile, but she wasn't in the mood for a heart-to-heart. Her ankle hurt like nobody's business. Not to mention the weight of a man's life was now on her shoulders.

She didn't know what the recourse of all this would be. No doubt there'd be some kind of investigation into Christophe's death. When her name came up, she hoped she had the strength to stand up for herself. Not to mention that there would be enough evidence to prove it wasn't her who had murdered him.

Doug rubbed his eyes. Was he frustrated this wasn't turning out like he had planned? Good. Immediately she wanted to take that thought back. Despite the imposing size of him, he did look sort of lost.

Sabine had enough to deal with without letting him distract her from her job, so she ignored him. She had the hard drive. It really was time to go before someone identified her. After dumping everything into the rolling carry-on she traveled with, she slipped her feet into silver flats, put her sunglasses on top of her head and turned to the door.

Doug grabbed her elbow, but she kept going. After a tug of war in which she lost her sunglasses and found herself sitting on the desk chair, she finally acknowledged him. He towered over her, his hands on the armrests.

Sabine lifted her chin. "Make this fast. I have a plane to catch."

"I'm coming with you."

Sabine almost swooned with the vulnerability in his tone. Almost. "I don't think so."

"Sabine, this is serious. Right now, where you go, I go. That's how it has to be."

"Why?"

"You're seriously asking me that? We have to figure out what just happened. You want to find Ben's killer? Well, so do I. If we pool our resources together, we have the best chance of that. So we're going to meet up with my team, and you're going to tell me what you're doing here, what you want with that hard drive you hid in your purse and whatever else you know."

She smirked. He thought she was going to spill everything just like that? Yep, amateurs. "Answers, answers. Let's see. Life…the universe…and forty-seven."

"Funny." He wasn't laughing. "I think you know something. Maybe it's a small thing…or maybe you're the key to all of this."

She sighed. "Am I supposed to know what on earth you're talking about?" He should know how it was. They both lived their lives under the radar. That was the whole point of being a spy. He was Special Forces. They only told the people closest to them what they did.

"I guess we'll find out."

Sabine glared. "Even if I could help you, there's no way

I would give you even one second of my time. You were there when my brother died—"

"I can't talk to you about that. It's classified."

"Look, MacArthur—"

"Doug."

Sabine rolled her eyes. "The only thing I care about is bringing whoever killed Ben to justice. Whatever association you and I might've had has now ended. Unless you care to share what happened that night."

The muscle at the corner of his eye twitched. "You need my help if you're going to get out of this hotel without getting questioned for Christophe's death."

"You said yourself we don't have much time before those two guys find us, or someone raises the alarm about Christophe being dead and the whole place swarms with cops."

He held out his hand. "Let's go then."

She brushed it aside and stood. "This is where we part. It's been an experience, really. But like I said, I have a plane to catch."

"Look, I know how hard this must be for you."

Was he serious? "You have no idea—"

"Let me finish." He had the decency to look apologetic. "Please. I can help you put this to rest, but I have to know how you fit in."

"You think I had something to do with Ben's death?" She forced the words past a resurgence of the complete and utter desperate, aching solitude that had followed her brother's death. To her horror, a slice of her private grief tracked its way down her cheek.

She swiped away the moisture and shoved past him.

"Try seeing this from my perspective, Sabine. The team is shadowing the man who paid for your brother to be executed—"

"Executed—" The word was a whisper from her mouth.

Doug winced. "We're trying to get to the bottom of it. You can help me find out what happened. If need be, we'll clear your name. We both want justice. Let's work together."

She shook her head. "I can't. Christophe is dead, and I plan on getting as far from this as possible. Unless there's something seriously incriminating on the hard drive that leads to the killer and lays out the whys of it all—which I seriously doubt—then it's over. My brother is dead. Justice is just a vain hope."

"Sabine—"

Her stomach churned. "No. I was wrong to attempt this. A man is dead. Yes, he was a criminal. And most likely responsible for Ben's death. That means in some way justice has already been served. Let's leave it there. Please. I'm going to turn the hard drive over to my handler and walk away."

Doug's eyes were wet. "I can't let you do that. I have to know what happened. I won't beg for your help, but I don't see how you can walk away and let this lie."

The heartbreak on his face nearly did her in. Sabine touched his cheek, feeling the warmth of his skin and the late-day stubble. "We need time to grieve. Both of us."

Something flickered in his eyes, and everything changed. She drew her hand away. Her stomach plunged like an elevator at the thought of exactly what that look might mean. But she couldn't let it penetrate the fortified walls of her heart.

For the first time, Doug was more than her brother's team leader. Despite what had brought them together, he was being a friend to her. Since she had few true friends, it was hard to recognize one or to trust the offer of friendship when it was given.

Ben had reacted…badly, when she had told him what she really did for a living. Granted, he'd been thrown after finally admitting to her what his position was in the army. *Delta Force.*

After he had told her that he was Special Ops, Sabine couldn't let the opportunity pass to open up about her own occupation. How was she to know he would hit the roof when he found out her job was just as dangerous as his—maybe more so, since she didn't have a team to back her up?

She didn't want to know what would have happened if Doug hadn't been there today. She'd needed him to get her out of Parelli's room after she realized she was going to be framed. So much for being a capable agent. Did that mean she couldn't handle this job on her own?

Doug pulled the cap from his head, ran his hand down his face and replaced his ball cap. "I'm sorry. You don't need the weight of my grief, too."

Sabine turned away and swiped up the handle of her suitcase. "Tensions are high. Don't sweat it."

"Sabine—"

"I told you I have a plane to catch."

Sabine was out of her depth. Sure, she was a trained agent. She was just more of an information-gathering, bug-planting, charm-the-bad-guy-into-talking kind of spy. She was about as far from a fully armed Special Ops team as it was possible to be, despite their mutual goal of finding out who had killed Ben.

Doug grabbed her arm. "I can't let you leave, Sabine. You're not going anywhere without me until I get some answers."

THREE

Mistakes. That's what it all boiled down to in Doug's mind. His life could be summed up in a series of mistakes that never should have been made—the most recent of which stood in front of him now. He touched her elbow. It was slender, her skin smooth under his rough fingers callused from a war he had never wanted to reach her shore.

Her head reached his chin, and her hair reflected every shade from auburn to dark chocolate. The red dress flattered her figure in a way that wasn't suggestive. She was pure class. The color looked warm against the almost Mediterranean-rich tan of her skin. Ben had been much lighter. Doug had wondered why the siblings hadn't looked anything alike. On the day he had asked Ben, Doug had been given a *back off* look. He didn't ask again.

Despite the feelings she evoked in him, Doug was on a mission, and emotions had no bearing. At least they weren't supposed to. He'd have to chalk up his earlier outburst to being overcome with grief. After all, who knew the extent of her involvement in Christophe Parelli's life, his business and his death? The quicker Doug got both of them out of here, the quicker he could find out how Sabine figured into Ben's death. CIA or not, she'd be answering a whole lot of questions.

After that she would be free to walk out of his life. He thought of all those get-togethers when he'd had to force himself to be cordial while everything in him hummed just from being near her. The reality of how shallow his attraction to her was hit him like a needle that burst a balloon and deflated his sense of honor.

It seemed like his initial impression had been entirely wrong. Not about her being very good at what she did. He'd believed she was some high-powered financial type at the bank where she worked. Ben had told anyone who would listen that his sister was a big deal, traveling all over the world for her job.

Had Ben even known the truth?

She wasn't the type of woman that Doug wanted to get to know. Even though just looking at her made his brain miss critical steps, Doug couldn't let her affect him. She'd charmed her way close enough to Christophe Parelli to get his fingerprints, and Doug had no interest in a woman who used her looks to get what she wanted. Once this mission was over, they'd both get on with their lives.

"My plane leaves in three hours." She lowered her slim wrist. The gold bracelet didn't look like any watch he'd ever seen. The smallest bit of fear crept on her face, despite the stubborn set to her shoulders.

"You'll be on it. Just as soon as we get to a safe place where you can answer some questions."

A click in his earpiece signaled California had something to say. "You gonna bring her over here, MacArthur?"

Doug caught her eye. How would she react to being crowded by army operatives? She knew each of them, except Ben's replacement. He'd seen her laugh and talk with the boys and their wives and girlfriends. Still, despite her status as a teammate's sister, he doubted any of them would be kind now that there were questions over her involvement.

"We'll be there in five, California."

He hoped the crack in her armor, the one currently giving off waves of fear, was an indication that she'd share what she knew. Doug had no intention of interrogating her. Nor could he hurt her in any way.

Even if it hadn't been Sabine, he wasn't the kind of man who did that. It didn't line up with what he'd been taught, his personal code of ethics or his faith. All in all, that was a lot of rules, but they were good rules. Honest standards he could live by and know he got things right.

Sabine Laduca was the antithesis of everything he stood for—a bolt of lightning. Would God create a woman for the sole purpose of throwing Doug off his game?

Well, he might be thrown, but there was no way she would bring him down.

If that tear she had tried to hide was anything to go by, he'd brought her grief back to the surface. There was no other choice. Doug was tempted to dial down his determination to find the truth. For the sake of this woman's obvious pain, he could take some extra time to soothe her into sharing.

But he wasn't going to.

Could she really be involved? Who even knew what the CIA was up to? In spite of his personal distaste, he had to push her. He couldn't afford to suddenly go soft. Sabine knew something. Until he found out what, she was going to have to deal with the discomfort. They were together. And she was right. They really shouldn't stay in this room any longer. Parelli's guys could show up again any second.

"You good to go?"

Sabine grabbed her roll-on suitcase again. But this time when she straightened, her face was a blank mask.

He sighed. "Right. Let's move."

He took the suitcase from her. She didn't like it, given the look on her face. Too bad. No man worth his salt made a woman pull her own suitcase when he was perfectly capable.

Doug scanned the hall both ways, gave a short nod and led her out, taking her hand to make sure she stayed with him. He paid no mind to the shimmer of warmth when he touched her slender fingers. He just hadn't held a woman's hand in a long time.

He pressed the button for the elevator. To anyone observing, they were simply a couple on their way down to check out. They could easily be on their honeymoon for all anyone else knew—except for the lack of wedding rings.

And didn't that just prick his heart in a way he wasn't ready to consider? Maybe, after he retired from the army, he could have that kind of relationship with a woman. Whoever she was, the woman he married would understand his driven nature because her heart beat to the same pattern. Family. Loyalty. Trust. Honesty. Those were the lifeblood of any relationship.

It was too bad he could never trust the woman beside him. His dream was just that—a dream. Until then he'd have to rely on God to take care of the future. The years of training that made him the man he was today would cover the here and now.

Six foot four, 250 pounds of muscle, Doug was a weapon honed by the United States Army into one of their best soldiers—a fact that had nothing to do with who his father was. Doug had sent home all the *daddy's boy* naysayers with their tails between their legs. Sure, Doug could have gone the West Point route and earned butter bars, but the gold bars of a lieutenant's rank would have put him behind a desk commanding missions. Not on the ground in the thick of it.

His dad had known exactly how hard Doug would have to work to push himself beyond his limits and earn the position of team leader. The general might have made Doug earn every patch the hard way, but it'd been worth it to feel the achievement of having done it. They understood that about each other, at least.

When the doors opened on the lobby, Doug tensed. Through the crowd of people milling around, he spotted his teammate assigned to the lobby—Franklin. Despite being in his late thirties, Franklin had the air of a middle-aged banker about him that allowed him to blend in anywhere.

Doug shifted his grip on Sabine's hand, and they strode to the front counter where she checked out of the hotel.

After signing *A. Surleski* on the receipt, she looked at him. "It's past lunch. I'm going to need something to eat pretty soon."

Doug looked her up and down. "You seem like a woman way too concerned about her appearance to be worried about something as pesky as eating."

Her eyes narrowed. "They do say that looks can be deceiving."

He doubted that. He knew her type. The expensive clothes said enough, but the way she held herself spoke much louder. He had a nagging feeling this woman was going to prove to be high maintenance when it served her purpose.

"In this case, I can read you loud and clear." He folded his arms across his chest. "But since I'm hungry, too, I guess we can rustle up something." He shot a look at the receptionist. The guy was busy typing into his computer. "After we join the others in our party and finish up our business, of course."

Her dangly gold earrings shook back and forth with the motion of her head. "There's a restaurant next door, remember? We can pick something up there."

"Oh, really?"

"Yes, really. I'm telling you—"

He stopped listening. The two guys who had chased them down the hall stepped off the elevator. "Time to go."

Doug strode to the side door, careful not to rush and draw anyone's attention. Dragged along by his grip, Sabine let out a yelp. He rolled his eyes and looked back. She made a valiant effort to keep up with his long strides. This had better be about her ankle. She'd better not be being difficult just because she wanted to go it alone.

The air outside was like stepping into a sauna. Doug quickened his pace, and heard a stir of noise and movement behind them. He cut right, pulled Sabine along the sidewalk and watched for a place to cross.

"They're coming." Her voice was a hiss. "They're right behind us."

He glanced back, and, sure enough, the men had exited the hotel and spotted them. With a shout, the suits started to run.

"Go. Now," Doug ordered.

A battered sedan pulled in front of them. Doug swerved, skirted the front bumper and glanced back. Franklin was nowhere to be seen, and the men were gaining on them.

"We're not going to make it," Sabine answered, but he was too focused on moving and on the voice in his earpiece to respond.

"Ten feet to your left. Yellow cab."

They climbed in before the driver even stopped.

"Drive." Doug threw a wad of cash onto the front seat, and the driver hit the gas pedal. "Airport."

The radio in his ear clicked. "Copy that. Party's over, friends. MacArthur, we'll see you back at the house."

With that, the team was dispersed to make their own way back to the U.S., where they would rendezvous on base for debrief.

Beside him in the cab, Sabine pulled her hand from his grip and rubbed her wrist. Doug ignored his heavy heart, even as it added to the measure of weight he already carried. What would Sabine say when she found out what he'd done? A woman like her would probably slap him across the face. He deserved it for his part in her brother's death.

He glanced out the back window. The two suited guys stood in the middle of the road outside the hotel. The bigger man formed his fingers into an imaginary gun, which he raised and fired at them.

Sabine flinched.

"We got away," Doug whispered, trying to reassure her. "They won't catch up to us again. I'll make sure of it."

She looked at him. "Because you're so good, you're certain? Wow, you're arrogant."

Doug shrugged, deliberately nonchalant. He needed answers from her. Needed her to talk and not retreat again. "It's true. I'm good at what I do. Once I have what I want, I'll be out of your life for good."

Sabine shifted away from him and kept her voice at a low whisper, too. "Don't make this out to be my fault."

"I stop at nothing to get a job done. It's very important you understand that. And to be doubly sure that we're clear? This is the most important thing I've ever done."

"It's my brother you're talking about."

He dipped his chin and leaned toward her. "Then we're on the same team. Only you want to walk away because your mission went wrong. Well, I don't give up that easily. I want the truth about what happened to Ben."

Sabine's eyes went wide. "I'm not giving you the hard drive."

"You think I care about salvaging your reputation? I couldn't care less about you saving face with your superiors or whoever it is you lone-wolf types report to."

"You just said we're on the same team."

He rolled his eyes again, this time to mask the fact he was impressed with the way she had twisted the conversation around and used his own words against him. "Does that mean you're going to help me find out who killed Ben and why?"

She stared at him for a good minute. "I'll help you."

He looked out the front window. The old man driving the cab alternately looked at the road and glanced back at them, probably straining to hear what they were saying.

"When we're back in the States, I'll tell you whatever I know."

Doug had a valid passport that was part of his government-issue cover identity and a credit card, so he could easily get a ticket on the same flight as Sabine. The problem was, he was suddenly in no hurry to rush back to the lengthy questioning sure to follow. And Sabine was hungry. If he fed her, maybe she would let him in now.

Doug tapped the driver on the shoulder. "We need food. Find us somewhere to eat."

The driver, who looked like the sun had baked him on high for too long, jerked his head up and down. "I take you to my mama's café. Best meal of your life."

"Good." Doug glanced at Sabine, who really shouldn't look that surprised. He was a nice guy. He handed the driver more money. "Make it fast."

Ten minutes later they pulled up outside a bleached building with a sign that read Mama's Café. After some discussion and more money, Sabine convinced the driver they needed to take her bag inside with them.

The ceiling fans did nothing to cut through the cloud of heat. The seats were faded vinyl, the tabletops were cracked and the air was saturated with the combined scents of breakfast and salsa. Doug's mouth watered and his stomach rumbled.

Sabine swept past him, pulling her suitcase, and glanced back over her shoulder. "Order me a burrito. Extra hot sauce." She disappeared into the women's bathroom.

An older woman with wrinkles, a faded polyester uniform and two missing teeth took his order. Doug slumped into the chair. Rested his forearms on the worn table. Toyed with the salt shaker. All the while he watched the door to the restroom.

He was just about to go searching when Sabine emerged. At least, he thought it was her. The woman who exited the bathroom dragging Sabine's suitcase looked completely different. She'd switched her dress for a white tank top adorned with two long necklaces and jeans tucked inside knee-high white leather boots. Big gold circular earrings hung down, and her hair had been swept up, wrapped in what looked suspiciously like a silk blouse he'd seen her pack in her suitcase.

She settled herself opposite him, pulled up the suitcase and put it on the seat beside her. Her whole demeanor was much more relaxed.

"Nice disguise."

She smirked. "Maybe the six-hundred-dollar dress was the disguise."

She frowned at him, and he noticed the gold watch bracelet was gone.

"It's a shame you don't have any other clothes with you," Sabine said.

"What's wrong with what I'm wearing?"

She grinned. "No offense, but you sort of stick out. Even though that outfit screams 'average-joe tourist.'"

He opened his mouth to object and realized she was probably right. He couldn't answer anyway because the waitress chose that moment to place their food in front of them.

"You could take off the hat," Sabine suggested.

He rubbed his shaved head and tugged the ball cap back on. "The hat stays."

"You don't have enough hair to have a bad hair day."

She picked up her silverware and cut a massive bite of burrito. His eyes widened as she shoved it in and chewed with gusto, then swiped up the bottle of hot sauce and shook a few drops onto her next forkful.

She realized he was staring and straightened. "What?"

He picked up his silverware. "Enjoy your food, don't you?"

"What's it to you?"

Doug shrugged. "It's just...refreshing is all. Women who look like you don't usually eat like, uh...that."

"I'll suffer working it off tomorrow, don't you worry. But it'll be worth the miles. Take a bite and see for yourself. It's really good."

Doug took a bite. She was right, though it was almost too spicy for him. He ate fast, one eye on the time. It would be simplest if they arrived at the airport with enough time for him to get a ticket on the same plane.

"So what's the real reason you don't want to take off your hat?"

He hesitated, unsure how to say it without dredging up a whole bunch of grief neither of them could handle. "It's—"

Sabine's knife stilled and sadness washed over her face. "That's Ben's hat."

Doug nodded.

"He gave it to you?"

"Wanted me to have it."

Sabine swallowed. "And here I only got the joy of cleaning out his musty, cluttered bedroom." She drew in a long breath, and he saw the quiver in her lower lip. "Not that I've done it yet. I mean, really, you'd think a grown man would be able to keep his room tidy. Especially someone in the military."

"You'd think that, what with all the spot inspections during basic training. Some guys pick up a tendency for order and bring it home with them. Others see their private living space as somewhere else to blow off steam."

"So what are you? A neat freak? Or does your place look like a tornado the way Ben's always did?"

"Does it matter?"

Sabine pulled away, any rapport they might have had now shut down by his tone. Doug had no intention of moving into personal territory with this woman. No matter how much he wanted to.

It was for the best.

He stood. "I'm going to make a pit stop, and then we should get going."

The bathroom looked about as good as it smelled. Doug held his breath and took care of business as fast as possible. What would his superiors say when he turned up with Sabine in tow? CIA operatives and the army didn't exactly mix. Talk about a clash of cultures.

He pushed open the door and glanced around the restaurant. His stomach sank. "You've got to be kidding me."

He rushed out the front door. The cab was gone, too.

She'd ditched him.

FOUR

Windshield wipers valiantly swiped the rain away, but more drops continued to pound on the car. Sabine parked her baby—a paid-in-full black Cadillac CTS—in the garage of her Seattle home. Only when the garage door lowered fully did she get out and pull her suitcase from the trunk.

It was late, and every muscle in her body ached, which was good because it distracted her from the throb in her ankle. Sabine had never been able to sleep on planes, and today was no exception. She tried to tell herself it was because she had felt bad for having ditched Doug. His tears had been genuine, the grief he had felt over Ben's death right there in his eyes. He clearly wanted to know what had happened as badly as she did—even if his professional manner left something to be desired.

There was still no way she was going to let him question her. She would need clearance from her handler before she could give him any of the details of her mission or tell him what she knew about Christophe Parelli.

The utter disaster the mission had turned out to be

weighed on her. Apart from the fact she had the hard drive, everything that could have gone wrong had. Hiding the hard drive from Doug had been necessary, though apparently pointless since he'd known what she was after.

Now she needed to go through the contents before anything else went awry—like being hauled in for questioning by the army.

Christophe's death played like a movie reel through her mind. Maybe she didn't need to feel bad since the man was responsible for the deaths of so many others. He had acted without remorse or any consideration for national and international laws. But seeing him gasp his last breath had hit Sabine at the very center of who she was.

Her house was dark and quiet, except for the patter of rain against the windows. That wasn't anything new—the Seattle weather or the solitude. Even when she was married, Sabine would come home to an empty house and dinner for one.

What she had thought was her husband's work as an investment banker keeping him busy with "late-night meetings" turned out to be Maxwell having drinks with his twenty-two-year-old secretary. Now Sabine was as alone as ever but with the added bonus of feeling like a chump because her husband had cheated on her with someone younger and prettier. She would think twice about letting anyone else in again.

She punched the first two numbers of her ten-digit code on the panel for the security system and paused. It wasn't armed. That was weird. She'd set it before she left, hadn't she? She never forgot something as important as security. Sabine set down her suitcase at the bottom of the stairs and stood still for a moment. The house was quiet as always.

After a walk-through of the downstairs rooms yielded nothing, Sabine crept upstairs, keeping to the side so as not to step on the creaky stair halfway up. Cold shimmered through her from head to toe. She had never needed a gun at home before. Her handler's words from the park came back to her.

Don't get caught with a gun. Ever. And don't get caught by the police, not even for a speeding ticket. You do and you're on your own.

Careful not to look at the pictures of Ben on the wall, Sabine rounded the stairs at the top and studied the upstairs hallway. Her ears strained for…a rustle coming from Ben's bedroom.

The door to her brother's room had been closed since his last day of leave and his subsequent return to base. He'd always been sort of juvenile about her going into his room, a response probably from the lack of privacy they'd had in foster homes. She'd respected his wishes and had agreed not to go in there.

Light flashed across the opening, and Sabine crept forward. She peered into the room and eased the door open inch by inch.

A black balaclava covered the intruder's face, leaving only his eyes visible. It was definitely a guy, judging by the shape of his wiry body. The efficiency with which he worked his way through Ben's belongings told her that he was a professional. This wasn't just some teenager looking to score.

He slammed the dresser drawer shut and yanked open the next one. A gun wouldn't scare off this guy and would likely raise more questions than she was okay with when she had to explain a dead body to the police.

She would have to rely on her CIA training.

Sabine took a deep breath and rushed him. He looked up a split second before she slammed into him with the force of her body and knocked him off balance. The guy twisted so she was the one who hit the floor and the back of her head slammed against the carpet.

Before she could react, his hands were on her neck. She tried to push him off, but his weight and the pressure on her windpipe made her see stars.

The doorbell rang downstairs.

With shaky hands she found his shoulders, then his face, where she applied pressure with her thumbs until he cried out. She kicked off the floor hard enough to dislodge him and dove for the dresser top for something to use as a weapon. Two arms locked around her waist and lifted her off her feet. Sabine cried out and was dragged backward.

A loud thud came from downstairs. "Sabine!"

She struggled against her captor. Strength bled from her like water down the drain but she lifted her legs and slammed until she made contact with the intruder's shins. He let go of her and collapsed to his knees.

Boots pounded up the stairs.

Sabine spun and caught the intruder with a kick to the side of his head. The pain in her twisted ankle nearly buckled her legs, but she followed up with a solid punch. The guy still hadn't gone down. In fact, he was regrouping.

The bedroom door swung open, hit the wall and bounced back. Doug filled the doorway. Despite the fact that she'd left him in the Dominican Republic, something inside her leapt at the thought that he'd come to help her, not interrogate her.

The intruder took one look at Doug and sprinted for the window. The smash was deafening. Sabine ran over and looked out, but he was already up on his feet and running across the lawn. Rain sprayed in through the open window and Sabine backed up from the broken glass.

Doug's phone beeped.

"What are you doing?"

"I'm calling the cops. What do you think I'm doing?"

Sabine tried to grab the phone, but he refused to let go of it. All the warmth she'd felt when he burst in like some kind of knight of yore here to save the princess in distress deflated like a pricked balloon. He was trying to tell her what to do again.

"No cops. There are too many things I don't care to explain about my life or why someone would break into my home." She lost her grip on the phone then, probably because it was soaked, like Doug's leather jacket, jeans and wool hat. "How long were you outside? You're drenched."

"How long does it take to cross the street?" He folded his arms.

Sabine loved the sound of leather crackling.

"Nice weather you guys have here."

"I like it. It discourages lingering."

He grinned. "Kind of antisocial, aren't you?"

"Why are you here?"

Instead of answering, he turned away, and Sabine followed him to the garage where he rummaged around her damp Cadillac and came up with a hammer, some spare pieces of two-by-fours Ben had left and a box of nails.

She stood at the bottom of the stairs, tapping her foot—even though it hurt. Halfway up he looked back over his shoulder. "I don't suppose you'll accept saving you from an intruder as an answer."

"Not likely, since I had it handled." Sort of.

As nice as it would be to believe he'd come here to help, he couldn't have known she'd need saving from an intruder at that very moment. Since Doug was busy fixing her window, Sabine headed into the kitchen for some water and to raid her stash of painkillers. She didn't dare sit. What little strength kept her upright now would dissipate, and she'd be asleep in thirty seconds. While she was incapacitated, Doug would probably throw her over his shoulder and take her to whoever he reported to for that questioning he'd threatened her with.

No, it wouldn't do to let her guard down.

Upstairs she could hear the thud of the hammer. The last time he'd been in this kitchen with her—at Ben's memorial service—he'd been nice. Now he was being nice again, helping her. He probably thought she couldn't have fixed it herself. He'd be right. She was so drained it was tough to think straight.

Was he friend or foe? Doug acted like he cared. Then in her hotel room he had seemed so determined to find out what had happened to Ben that he was like a runaway train. Nothing would keep him from getting what he wanted.

She was a workaholic, but it seemed more like Doug lived and breathed the army. Now that this particular mission had become personal, there was nothing he wouldn't do.

Sticking around was a bad idea.

Sabine had just about summoned up the strength to figure out where her purse was when Doug reappeared, wiping his hands on the leg of his jeans.

"Thinking about running again?"

"I was—" Her voice gave out. Sabine touched her throat. It was tender from the intruder's grip. She sucked in a deep breath. In that moment it was all she had the strength to accomplish.

"Sabine."

His voice sounded far away, like he was speaking underwater.

The floor swept up toward her, and Sabine descended into darkness.

Doug caught her before she hit the floor and lifted her into the cradle of his arms. She weighed more than he thought. Tall and slender, Sabine was lean with muscle. Strong. The woman might have an iron core, but his heart had been in his throat since he'd been on her doorstep and heard her cry out over the sound of wind and rain.

After he had kicked the door in and pounded up the stairs, he'd been scared to death he'd find her dead on the floor. Instead, Sabine had put up a valiant fight against her assailant. Now rather than being outside searching for the guy who'd had the audacity to put his hands on Sabine—Doug had seen the marks on her throat—he carried her upstairs.

Doug set her down on the bed and removed her boots. Her ankle was puffy and swollen, but her breaths were deep and steady. He wrapped her in the comforter, turned on the bedside lamp and left the door ajar in case she cried out.

He sighed and lowered himself to the top step in the dark. He had to get a handle on his emotions. He couldn't freak out like that every time Sabine was in danger.

Pictures lined the wall, all the way down the stairs. He didn't need light to see the images of Ben at Little League or Ben wearing a tux as he walked Sabine down the aisle. She was divorced now. Ben had revealed that much about his sister, though none of the actual details—so long as you didn't count the way his lip curled when he mentioned Sabine's now ex-husband.

All Doug wanted was to find out who had killed Ben and why. After that he wouldn't have to wonder where she was or what she was doing…or if she wondered the same thing about him. Or what that sadness behind her eyes was.

His phone hummed. "Richardson."

"You got her?" The voice was gruff and full of authority, the voice of his commanding officer, Colonel Hiller.

"Found her fighting off an intruder in her house. Soon as she comes around, we'll be on our way."

There was a noncommittal noise. "She okay?"

Doug stood. He stretched out his back and made his way down the stairs. "She took some hits, but mostly she's just exhausted."

"I'm not surprised. That girl's one busy little beaver. Been up to all kinds of things since Sergeant Laduca died."

Doug's heart clenched at the memory of Ben bleeding out in his arms and forced himself to focus instead on his commanding officer's words. "She has?"

"Stuck her nose into classified records, for one thing. Girl's got a lot to answer for. The least of which being who she works for."

Doug found a diet soda in the fridge. It would have to do. "She's CIA."

"Not according to anyone I spoke to. Once upon a time, sure. They hired her, trained her and sent her on missions. A half dozen years ago she went off the grid. Disappeared, and the only thing she left behind was a pool of blood."

"She's some kind of rogue ex-CIA agent? Are you serious?" Then he remembered who he was talking to. "Excuse me, Colonel. I'm just having trouble assimilating this. She was kind of stuck-up about the CIA thing. If she works for someone else, she must be the best actress in the world." He thought for a second. "Did you tell the CIA we found her?"

"They're not stupid. Mostly. They'll figure out why I was asking about her, even though I did my best to keep it to vague questions. Hopefully it'll buy us time."

Doug tapped his finger on the side of the sweating can of soda. He wasn't going to tell Sabine what they'd found out. He'd probe instead with the hope that she would share of her own volition. Had Ben known she was a rogue agent? Doug had to get to the bottom of this before it all broke loose.

If she had betrayed the CIA and gone to work for the enemy six years ago, the CIA would have her on all kinds of watch lists. To have hidden her location and still be going on missions, fooling everyone left, right and center, meant she must be an exceptional spy. That or she worked for some very bad people…with very deep pockets.

A rogue CIA agent?

Doug sighed and ran a hand down his face.

"Get some answers, Sergeant Major. I expect to hear from you bright and early."

"Yes, sir."

"And call your dad."

Doug groaned.

"The old man knows you're back in the States. He's expecting your call."

The line went dead. Colonel Hiller wasn't one for goodbyes or any kind of politeness that could be expected from a fellow human being, but his record as an officer was so impressive; he was already a legend at forty-six. He'd earned his rank the hard way, from the ground up—ground soaked with his own sweat and blood.

Doug found a can of soup in the cupboard and set about heating it up on the stove. He scrolled through his contacts, found "Andrew" and pressed Send, intending to leave a voice mail.

"General Richardson's residence."

Doug smiled at the sound of the housekeeper's voice. "Hey, Jean. I take it he's still up since it's after midnight, yet you're answering the phone."

The fluffy middle-aged lady laughed like Doug's old Sunday school teacher. "How are you, honey?"

"I'm doing fine, Jean. Thank you."

"Well, you know I worry about you. Did you get those cookies I sent?"

"I did, yeah. They were good. The guys loved them." He'd made sure to set aside some of the two dozen for himself.

"I should think so."

Doug laughed. The lightness in him stretched and grew, even with such a small connection with someone who had nothing to do with the war he seemed to always be fighting.

"My grandmother's secret recipe. Did you know she fought her way out of Nazi Germany with nothing but her recipe card box and her knitting needles?"

Laughter built up in his chest but didn't spill out. "That's a good story. You should stick with it."

"I'll do that. I'll put you through to your dad now, honey."

"Thanks, Jean."

There was a pause, and then a man's voice came over the line. "That you, son?" It was a voice that had both commanded troops and yelled at his teenage boy to straighten his room.

Doug sighed. "Yeah, Dad, it's me."

"It's about time. Did you think I'd settle for you checking in over voice mail forever?"

Doug's chest tightened until it ached. He should pay the old man a visit soon. "It's late. I should probably let you get to bed."

"Don't even try it. This is a momentous occasion. I actually got you on the phone. You think I'm just going to let you say goodbye in two seconds? Besides, isn't there something you want to tell me?"

Doug sighed, loud enough for his dad to hear. Of course he'd make him say it. "Happy birthday."

"You want to make it happy? You show up at my birthday party on Saturday. You wear a tux. You smile. You tell me that you're letting this whole business go." His voice broke. "I want to see you get on with your life, Douglas. Find a woman. Get married, and make me a grandfather already. I'm getting old."

Before the general was finished, Doug was already shaking his head. "I would if I could, but I can't. Not until I find out who killed Ben."

"It's not just me. You know it's what your mother would have wanted."

"Oh, sure." Doug sighed. "Bring up Mom and how she'd be so disappointed in my behavior." His dad did it because it worked. Doug would never have willingly disappointed his mother.

The general huffed. "Always were too hard on yourself."

"This isn't just about me."

"I get it, son. I do." Fatigue clouded the old man's voice. "You want justice for your friend so your team can go on."

"And for his sister."

"You want to protect her."

"She's strong, but she still seems so…fragile."

There was quiet for a moment and then the general asked, "Is she pretty?"

"Dad."

"Fine, fine. You do what you need to do, son. But when you're done, you come see me, you hear?" The general waited a beat. "I miss you."

Doug pressed End and lowered the phone. "I miss you, too."

FIVE

The first clue that told Sabine something was off was when she woke up in bed fully clothed. Sun streamed through the open curtains and dust danced in the beam. The lamp beside her bed was on, so she switched it off and winced as various twinges made themselves known.

She staggered into the bathroom, dreaming so strongly of coffee she thought she could smell it. Only when she was submerged to her chin in a bath that was more soap bubbles than water did she relax. But she wasn't truly clean until she brushed her teeth, put on yoga pants and a stretchy pink top, and blow-dried her hair.

The soft carpet on the stairs felt nice between her toes. There was something she was supposed to be thinking about. Lots of things, probably; heavy things that made her heart squeeze in her chest. She closed her eyes and turned the corner at the bottom of the stairs, concentrating on the smooth wood of the banister under her fingers.

Until she had coffee she wasn't going to let anything bother her. At least anything more than why it seemed as if the coffee had already been made. Now that she thought about it, it sort of smelled like someone had cooked, too. Under the coffee scent, there was onion and cheese.

Her stomach rumbled.

This must be a dream. No one ever made the coffee except her, and she hadn't had a hot breakfast in years. She always had bland, tasteless cereal. But she wasn't dreaming—there was a dark figure behind the frosted glass of her kitchen door. She tried to inhale but the air got stuck in her throat, and she could feel the press of the intruder's hands around her neck.

"Are you going to get in here or just stand in the hall all day?" Doug opened the door. The smile on his face dropped, and he reached for her. "Sabine—"

She raised both hands. "Don't."

He moved aside for her. She didn't want to decipher the look on his face; it would invite too many questions about why he was in her kitchen. Cooking breakfast. Sabine lifted the lid on the pan and groaned. Sure enough, there was an omelet in there and it was covered in cheese. There hadn't been anything in the fridge last night.

"I went to the store this morning."

She must have spoken aloud. Her cheeks warmed, and Doug smiled like he was indulging her. She narrowed her eyes. "You weren't worried I'd take off while you were gone?"

"Figured it was worth the risk." He poured a cup of coffee and handed it to her. "You want creamer or half-and-half? I wasn't sure how you drank your coffee, so I got both."

Sabine took the cup for the peace offering it seemed to be. Why was he being nice to her? Was it just because he'd seen her when she was vulnerable and unable to take care of herself? Well, he could get over that. It wasn't going to happen again if she had anything to say about it.

She went to the fridge and got the fat-free milk. "I thought you just wanted answers."

He divided the omelet into two pieces with a spatula,

one bigger than the other. "I figured I'd get further if you didn't pass out again."

"I did not pass out."

He looked up. "What do you call it then?"

Sabine turned away and got forks from the drawer. Doug got the message and put their breakfast on two plates.

"It was nothing more than a spontaneous reaction to stress."

She thought he might have snorted. When she was about to give him what for, he held out the plate with the smaller portion. Sabine grabbed the bigger one from his other hand and walked to the table with her prize.

Doug waited until she was finished before he pushed his empty plate aside. He folded his hands together on top of the table.

She frowned. "This looks serious."

"It is serious."

Her shoulders drooped and she sighed. "I guess I have to face the real world eventually. It was nice to forget about it for a while, even if it was fleeting. Thank you for making breakfast."

Did she know she was running her nail along a grain in the tabletop?

"No one's ever done that for me before."

He tried not to look surprised. Her husband hadn't ever cooked her breakfast? "It was my pleasure."

"But now business?"

"Sorry." He wasn't sure why he apologized, as though that would combat any of the guilt. She seemed so small across the table from him, he had to resist the urge to cover her hand with his. "I still think we should work together, Sabine. As I said before, we both want to find out who killed Ben and why. It makes sense to pool our resources and team up. We'll work quicker that way."

"Okay." She didn't lift her gaze from the table.

"That's it? You're not going to fight me on this?"

"Why would I? It makes sense. We do want the same thing. The quicker we get to the bottom of this, the better off we'll both be."

He couldn't disagree with that. The guilt of not being able to save Ben ate at Doug like a stomach ulcer. If he could make enough sense of it to move on, he'd be a lot happier. He'd have peace. Sabine looked like she could use some peace, too.

"So where do we start?"

Doug stood and grabbed both their plates. "The dishes?"

Her eyes narrowed, but she followed him to the sink where he rinsed and she put things in the dishwasher. "Is this some weird way of buttering me up? You come here and play house with me while you try to get me to spill what I know? Is this your attempt at torture?"

He snorted. "If I had decided to torture it out of you, I'd hardly do it by making breakfast. I'd probably withhold food, knowing how much you like it."

"Shame you didn't think of that earlier. It probably would have worked." She waltzed to the door. "Too bad you'll never know what I'd have told you."

"Sabine." He caught up with her at the bottom of the stairs. "We need a plan."

"I'm going to get dressed. That's the plan."

"Then what?"

She looked at him like he didn't have a clue. "When I'm wearing real clothes and I've put on makeup, then we'll look through Ben's things and try to find out why someone was in there snooping."

Doug watched her walk away and tried to figure out

how he was going to get out of this without Sabine leaving him twisted in knots. He didn't think she realized the effect she had on him.

It had been hard for him to think straight when she walked in the kitchen. The look on her face when she realized he'd made breakfast almost broke his heart. The loneliness there was the mirror image of how he felt every time he let himself into his apartment and recalled it was just him living there alone.

Too bad relationships were something he'd never had success at. He'd definitely enjoy seeing Sabine dressed up and taking her out to dinner. She needed to smile more; she needed someone to treat her the way she deserved to be treated.

You don't love me. You only love your job.

Tara's voice echoed in his thoughts and reminded him of the reason he couldn't start something with Sabine. Not even considering what she'd say when she found out he was responsible for Ben's death, there was too much going on in the world. Too much evil to fight for Doug to be less than 100 percent committed to his job. Relationships took too much of the energy he needed on missions. He couldn't get distracted thinking about getting home to her, or then his dad would get a call saying Doug had been killed in action.

When Sabine realized he wouldn't give up his job, her heart would get broken and since he couldn't stand to see her hurt, that meant she was off-limits.

She came into view at the top of the stairs wearing pressed black trousers and a blue buttoned-up blouse. Apparently "real clothes" meant she had to look like she worked a regular nine-to-five job in an office.

"We should look at the hard drive you took from Christophe."

She opened her mouth and closed it again. "I'll get it after we go through Ben's room."

Satisfied she might not hold out on him, he looked through the drawers and under Ben's bed while Sabine checked the closet. The shelf above where Ben's clothes hung was a jumble of shoe boxes, canvas bags and blankets that looked like they'd been stuffed up there.

Under the bed was a mess of food wrappers and dirty clothes Doug didn't dare touch. The drawers were disturbed the way you'd think, since someone had broken in and pawed through it all. Then again, when Ben had grabbed his things and left for base the last time, it probably looked much the same.

"Not the neatest person in the world." Doug glanced at Sabine, cross-legged on the floor and rifling through a shoe box filled with old photos. She covered her mouth with her hand, and he realized she was trying not to cry.

He crouched beside her. "What is it?"

She looked up, her eyes wide. "Pictures. Old ones." She handed one to him. Two little kids—Sabine and Ben around elementary school age by the looks of it.

"That your parents?" A good-looking couple had their arms around the kids, and everyone was smiling.

Sabine nodded. "I never even knew he had these."

"You guys look happy."

"I guess. We were in foster care by the end of that year."

There was something in her voice, a guardedness which told him that she wasn't convinced there was happiness behind the smiles. "What happened?"

Sabine stuffed the photos back in the box. "It doesn't matter now. Let's keep looking."

"Ben wouldn't tell me what happened, either."

She tried not to let him see her flinch, but he caught it. "I'm surprised he even remembered. He was little, and we never talked about it. They tried to get us to see counselors, but it wasn't anyone else's business. We moved on." Her eyes filled. "And now he's gone."

"It won't always feel like this. It'll ease."

She shook her head. "I don't want it to ease. If the pain goes away, it means I'm forgetting him."

"It's okay to heal, Sabine."

"Sounds like you know."

"I've lost brothers in combat before. It doesn't get easier, but you learn how to deal with it. Some of the guys drink too much. Some blow off the steam of their grief in other ways. You have to, or you'll bottle it up until one day you explode."

She looked up at him. "What do you do?"

"I run. And I pray while I run."

Sabine pulled away from him for the second time. He didn't know where she stood on the whole faith thing, but Ben had been a new Christian before his death. Time and again Doug had caught the younger man eyeing Doug over something he had said or done. One night when they were alone on a mission, Ben had asked Doug why he was different than the other team members.

Two days later Ben had announced to Doug his commitment to follow Jesus.

Two weeks after that, Doug had held Ben's body while Ben took his last breath.

Ben's commitment to the Lord was the one good thing in this whole mess. Sabine had loved her brother. Eventually Doug would have to tell her that it was his fault that Ben was dead, and Doug might as well have pulled the trigger himself.

When she found out, it would kill everything that was between them.

It didn't look to him like she was over any of it. Whatever had happened to her parents was fresh in her mind still. Not that he could talk. He had plenty of issues. "Surely you told your husband about what happened to your parents when you got married?"

She looked at him as if he'd grown two heads. "Don't presume you know anything about me or my marriage. That part of my life is not up for discussion."

Doug wasn't about to back down. "We're not going to get anywhere in this partnership if we can't trust each other."

"That doesn't mean I'm going to share everything with you. All we're doing is finding out who killed Ben. My personal life has nothing to do with it."

"I'm not saying that." Because there was a whole lot he was never going to share. "All I'm saying is there has to be some give and take here."

She folded her arms. "Fine then, you go first."

He sat in the chair at Ben's desk, ready to be grilled. "Fire away."

"Have you ever been married?"

"Almost, a long time ago."

"What happened?"

Doug took a deep breath. "She decided I loved my job more than I loved her."

"Did you?"

"Probably." He didn't feel guilty. It had saved him from getting tied down in a bad situation. He'd have been miserable as Tara's husband. "I do a tough job, one that takes all my attention. There's not a lot left over for a wife."

"That's a total cop-out. Soldiers get married every day. Sure, it's hard to keep a good marriage together, but that goes for everyone. There's added pressure because you're gone so much. I think, if you had wanted it to work, you'd have figured it out."

"Is that what happened to you?"

Sabine flinched. "That was a totally different situation."

"I know, I know." He raised his palms. "Don't presume I know you. But I'd like to. We need to build some trust between us."

He watched her compose herself, like a new recruit facing battle for the first time—trying to hide the fear.

"With Maxwell and me, it was different. There wasn't a lot of affection between us in the first place. That didn't change much after we got married. I mistakenly thought the sense of security that came with being married would make up for it. When he took up with his secretary, I didn't see much point in letting the farce continue."

Doug couldn't believe a man married to Sabine hadn't been totally committed to making their lives together a rich and enjoyable experience. She deserved that much. He wanted to ask why she had settled for a marriage like that, but she cut him off.

"We should take a look at the hard drive I got from Christophe."

Sabine stomped down the stairs. Why had she said all that? She had never talked about her marriage, not even to Ben. He hadn't been under any illusions about it, but he also had never questioned her decision to get married or said anything when she had filed for divorce.

Up until now she would have said she was over the whole experience. The look on Doug's face made her rethink that idea. Compassion, pity—whatever it was—made her uncomfortable. She'd rather walk away and not look back. She'd prefer he hadn't known anything of her bad decision to marry Maxwell. It hadn't really been a matter of her settling for less. A more loving relationship just wasn't something that she deserved.

Now it was so over, the divorce papers had dust on them. She couldn't have the kind of relationships other women seemed to think were so great. It wasn't in Sabine to be so vulnerable that it gave someone else the power to break her heart.

Sabine fished the hard drive from her suitcase and went into her office, proud that Doug would see her sanctuary.

The bookshelves heaved with everything from books on gardening—one day she'd do that—to popular classics. She didn't buy first editions; she bought books she could read again and again, ones that were now frayed. Some had tape on their spines they were so worn out. Just like the armchair. She'd spent many hours in the plush chair by the window, lost in another world.

Even though she'd rather go AWOL in any one of her books, she took the hard drive to the oak desk and slid it in the port that would download the contents to her desktop computer. In minutes they would have everything they needed to bring down the person responsible for Ben's death.

She switched on her computer and tapped her finger while it booted up. Doug scanned the shelves and made short noises. Was that good or bad?

He looked over at her. "You're pretty good with computers?"

Sabine exhaled. They were out of sensitive waters and back to plain old banter. "Who do you think taught Ben everything he knew?"

Doug looked impressed. Sabine shifted in the leather chair. A few clicks later, she tapped her fingers on the desk while the information downloaded.

"Sabine." Doug hauled her out of the chair, his eyes on the hard drive she'd flown halfway around the world for. Smoke curled up from the bay.

It sparked.

Doug pulled her to the doorway.

A loud boom shook the room. The force of the explosion blew her to the ground, and Doug landed on top of her. His head hit the floor beside her, and she winced at the sound.

Smoke filled the room. Sabine felt the heat of flames but couldn't move. Doug seemed to be unconscious, pinning her to the floor. "Get off me."

She shoved at him. "Get up, Doug." He didn't respond. Heat touched her bare foot. She tried to shift away from the flames, but couldn't move under his weight.

"Come on, soldier. Wake up. I have no intention of burning to death with you lying on top of me."

SIX

"I'm sorry I yelled at you when you were unconscious," Sabine said.

The fire truck pulled away from the house. She was beside him on the front step. Thankfully the blaze had been small and quickly contained, but Doug's head continued to thump from his injury, like he'd been hit with a brick. "I'm sorry I was unconscious."

"It could have been a lot worse." She raised her chin from the cocoon of the blanket the EMTs had given her. "It could still be raining."

Doug shrugged. "I guess."

"You don't really feel guilty about this, do you?" She laid a hand on his arm. "Doug, this wasn't your fault. You didn't know the hard drive would blow up. It's not your fault you were knocked out. We're both barely hurt."

"I know."

"But you should have…what? Done more? Cut yourself some slack. You're not a superhero, so far as I know. Just a regular human like the rest of us."

How was it she could take one look at him and deftly nail his problem? Was it so obvious he was plagued by guilt? He was just trying to do a good job, and things kept getting messed up.

A familiar prickle teased the back of his neck. Doug stood. They shouldn't be out in the open in broad daylight now that emergency services were gone. Too bad it was Saturday. When the front window of her office had blown out, her neighbor had been mowing his lawn. Good that the firefighters had come so fast; bad that many neighbors were home on the weekend and curious about the small explosion.

Doug was just glad he'd come to before the fire spread and thus had saved himself the indignity of being hauled out of the house by a firefighter.

"What is it?" Sabine looked up and down her street.

"It's not safe to stay here."

Her eyes flashed like she was getting ready to argue.

"Sabine—"

"I'm not disagreeing with you. I just have to get some things together before I can leave."

He held open the front door for her. "Pack for a few days. And bring anything of Ben's you think might yield information."

Sabine tore her eyes from the charred, waterlogged floor and the ash-covered walls. "Where are we going?"

"When I know, I'll tell you."

She ascended the stairs. Doug pulled out his phone and made a call.

"Colonel Hiller? The hard drive we got from Parelli had some kind of fail-safe. It blew up before we could get anything from it."

Kids screamed and laughed in the background. "I'm going to assume it's you who got the cops to back off with their questions."

"You're welcome, Sergeant Major. What's your plan?"

"Get her somewhere safe. Get some answers."

"Why don't the two of you head to your dad's place?"

There was silence for a moment. "You can't tell me the general wouldn't be fine with it. Not to mention he has the most secure residence we know of."

Doug fought the urge to reach through the phone and throttle his superior officer. "You're right, but I don't like it, sir."

"Want me to make it an order?"

Doug sighed. "Is this some kind of conspiracy to get me to his birthday party?"

The colonel barked a laugh and then yelled at his son to stop trying to drown his sister in the pool. "Birthday aside, it wouldn't hurt you to visit the man. He calls just about every day asking after you."

"His clearance is still good?"

"You think I tell him what you're doing?"

"Thank you, sir."

"You're welcome, Sergeant Major. Get yourself on a plane to D.C. Your dad's place will give you the space and the time you need to question Ms. Sabine Laduca. I'll get to tell the CIA that she's in our custody, and they can wait until we're done with her."

Doug wanted to ask all the questions on the tip of his tongue, but Sabine appeared. She hauled two huge suitcases down the stairs. "Yes, sir."

She glanced at him. Doug hung up the phone and she came to him, looking like she expected him to tell her who was on the phone and the content of the conversation.

"Got everything?"

"I'll put these in my car and come back for my purse and lock up the house."

She didn't get his sarcasm, apparently. "Actually, they're going in my rental car." He pointed out front. "The Prius across the street."

Her head cocked to the side. "I would have pegged you more as a big truck kind of guy."

She was right. "It was all they had." He grabbed the first suitcase. "Enough stalling—let's get moving."

By the time he crammed both suitcases alongside his duffel bag in the trunk of the tiny car, Sabine had locked her front door. He scanned the street while she crossed to him, looking good enough he needed to concentrate on something else or he'd get distracted. She might have a smudge of ash on the side of her face, but she was still beautiful.

In the car, Sabine buckled her seat belt. "So where are we going?"

He looked over. She was trying to hide a smirk. The driver's seat was a tight fit for him.

"Want me to drive?"

"No, thank you." He didn't care if his tone was short. "We're going to my dad's place in Washington. Gates, security guards, few people to worry about and plenty of space to sit down and figure all this out."

He drove out of her subdivision, pulled onto the freeway and headed for the airport. "Nothing to say?"

She just stared out the window.

"You're just going to let me take you wherever I want and not do anything about it?" They both knew she could give him the slip whenever she wanted. Doug would have to be on guard. "Sabine?"

She finally looked at him. "Take the next exit. I need something from my storage unit before we leave town."

He couldn't read the look on her face because he had his eyes on the road. Sometime soon they needed to sit down and have this out. There was still way too much he didn't know about Sabine, Ben and this whole business.

But there was something he needed to get clear right then. "Why did you tell me you were with the CIA?"

* * *

Sabine blinked and her face creased into a frown. "You think I was lying?"

"Were you?"

"Let me guess. You called to check my story?"

"My commanding officer did."

She nodded. "The CIA is supposed to deny my existence. It's what they do."

"I'm not so sure."

"Tell me what it is."

He glanced at her, and she saw a flash of worry had darkened his eyes. Interesting, since he didn't care about her. The only reason they were together was so he could interrogate her.

"The CIA claims you don't work for them anymore. Since six years ago, you've been a rogue agent."

Six years ago?

Sabine flinched. She could still feel the sting of gunfire from that day. With her cover blown, she'd been given a new handler and now worked in a clandestine department. Well, it was the CIA, so all the departments were clandestine, but hers even more so.

One day she'd either retire or end up as a nameless star on a wall, with only a handful of people who would ever really know what had happened to her.

Of course they would deny her existence. To them she probably didn't exist. That was the nature of the work she did. She didn't need to prove herself to Doug; she knew who she worked for. The fact that she hadn't even stepped foot inside Langley in those six years only proved just how under the radar they wanted her.

Doug pulled up outside a garage-size unit in the far corner of the complex. He could tell the news about who she worked for was a shock, but she seemed to push it away. The closer they drove to her storage area, the tenser she became.

With one foot out the parked car, she turned back. Her mouth was thin. "Stay here."

He watched her walk away. He wanted to go, despite what she said. He gripped the steering wheel so tight he was probably warping it. Sure, she'd ditched him yesterday in the Dominican Republic, but since then they'd fought off an intruder together and had almost been blown up. This was a good time to show her that he would do what she asked. Especially when she said it with that look of total despair on her face—the same look she'd had at Ben's funeral. She'd been ready to lose it to her grief again. What had brought it back to the surface now?

Her family had been happy at one time. At least if the photo in Ben's room was anything to go by. Then something had gone down, and the two of them had ended up in foster care until Sabine had turned eighteen and won custody of her fifteen-year-old brother. Doug had figured their parents were dead, but they could have just as easily been in jail.

Perhaps the loss of her brother was surging up at the most unexpected moment to blindside her, just as it did to him. Ben was the only family she had and Doug had taken that away from her. As if he had forgotten his culpability.

Doug watched Sabine stride past the unit number she'd given him, the one he would have been able to see directly into. She went three units down, unlocked it and slid up the door. Doug swallowed. He could pretend otherwise, but he had it bad when a woman using all her strength to open a garage door got to him.

He tapped the steering wheel.

Checked his phone.

Sabine reappeared with a briefcase, which she set on the backseat. She clipped her seat belt and looked up. "What?"

"You're not going to tell me what that is?"

"It's a briefcase."

"Sabine—"

"Oh, don't say it like you're so exasperated. I'm tired, Doug. It's been a rough couple of weeks. Can we at least try to be civil to each other for a while?"

"Fine. Only because I'm tired, too. Your couch is not the most comfortable place in the world to sleep. Though, I have bunked down in a lot worse places."

"You didn't use the guest room?"

"You passed out. I wasn't going to snoop around. I figured crashing on the couch was the least imposing way of keeping an eye on you."

"Keeping an eye on—"

"Enough." Doug held up his hand. "Let's go back to the truce. I liked that idea."

Sabine folded her arms. "Truce."

"Good. It won't be long, and then we can rest on the plane. When we get to my dad's, there might be a little party going on, but we can sneak in through the kitchen."

The *little party,* as Doug had put it, turned out to be a seventieth birthday bash for his father, General Andrew Richardson. Limousines lined the driveway. The entire place was lit up, and swing music from a live band poured out open windows. Doug drove their rental car—a midsize sedan this time—around the side of the house, through a brick archway to a rear courtyard.

Sabine wished she was wearing the green floor-length gown she'd put in her suitcase on a whim. A formal dress could come in handy at any time and packing for any occasion had long been a habit. Then again, anything would be

better than showing up in ash-smeared clothes and smelling like she'd run a marathon. At least she'd taken some
time at the airport to find a bathroom and clean up a little
bit. Though she'd have paid money for a shower.

"Ready?"

She nodded. Doug had valiantly tried to draw her into
conversation during the flight, but she hadn't been able to
get past the mess of thoughts that had hummed in her head
like a swarm of bees. Ben's death, then Christophe's, and
the loss of any leads they might have had. It was late, and
Sabine was ready for sleep. Maybe one day in the future
she'd wake up and not feel just as tired as she had when
she had gone to bed. As hard as she had pushed to find out
what had happened to Ben, it had taken its toll.

Doug got out the bags and opened her door. "You okay?"

"You mean other than smelling like a gym sock?"

He snorted. "You're so pretty I don't think that would
make a difference."

He thought she was pretty?

"Come on." He helped her out.

"I usually don't need this much babying."

"You said it yourself. It's been a rough time for you
lately."

"I don't like being helpless."

Doug snorted, pulling her bags by their handles, his
duffel hanging over his shoulder. "Whatever you are, Sabine Laduca, it's anything but helpless."

The door opened to an older woman with a stylish bob
cut and blond highlights. She was comfortably round in
her knit sweater and black slacks, and smiled wide at the
sight of them. "I didn't dare believe it until I saw it myself."

Doug dropped the luggage and swept her up into a hug.
"Jean." He kissed both her cheeks.

"The prodigal son returns."

Doug laughed. "I haven't been that bad, have I?"

The older lady chuckled. "He's done okay. Don't worry yourself."

"You take good care of him."

"Yes, yes." She ushered them into an extensive galley kitchen. "I'm more concerned with what you've brought with you, or should I say, whom?"

Sabine held out her hand. "Sabine Laduca."

"I know, darling. I'm Jean Pepper." The hand that clasped hers wasn't altogether soft, but it was warm. Sabine imagined the woman was much like a grandmother should be and had to push away a pang of something she didn't want to think about.

"Your brother had nothing but good things to say about you."

Sabine sucked in a breath, not knowing what to say. A lot of Ben's attachment to her had been because of what had happened to their parents. She'd loved Ben, but it was strange to meet someone who knew of her. So much for living a low-key life.

Thankfully Doug came to her rescue. He probably read her discomfort. Why he felt it necessary to put his hand on the small of her back was anyone's guess. Still, it was nice to have him stand shoulder to shoulder with her almost like they were a team. "I'm going to show Sabine upstairs so she can settle in."

Jean glanced between them as though she knew a secret. "Your tux is hanging from the closet door in your room."

"Does he know I'm here?"

"I decided to surprise him. He'd have been disappointed if you hadn't come."

Doug nodded to Jean and grabbed all the bags again. "I'll be back down shortly."

Sabine didn't offer to carry any of the bags. He'd been

adamant the few times she had tried to pull even one, giving her some ridiculous spiel about being perfectly capable. Apparently he didn't get that she was just as able.

Doug led her up a wide staircase with rich red carpet, wood paneling and portraits on the walls. The whole place was permeated with the musk of old money, while the bulk of her childhood consisted of mediocre foster homes, some not as nice as others. Sabine liked nice things, but this place made her want to take her shoes off at the door.

They passed a ballroom filled with glitzy people. When Doug cleared his throat, Sabine blinked and hurried to catch up. "Did you grow up here?"

He shook his head as they climbed. "We moved around a lot—you know, military family and all. When my dad got promoted and assigned to the Pentagon, we stayed. I was sixteen."

His voice had cracked. She waited until he was ready to say more.

"That was the summer my mom died." Their eyes met. "Her cancer snuck up on all of us, and it was over almost as fast as it had come."

"I'm sorry." What else could she say?

At least he had a mom for that long. Sabine had neither parent and barely remembered more than the last day they'd all been together, though she'd been nine. That day was still etched into her brain, never to be erased.

Doug left her in a room that was feminine but not over-the-top, with floor-to-ceiling drapes and a four-poster bed. He walked away muttering about simpering crowds and being choked by his own collar.

She smiled. Too antsy to rest, despite being exhausted, Sabine decided Doug might need some moral support downstairs. After all, there was a formal dress in her bag.

She headed for the bathroom.

* * *

Fresh from his four-minute shower, Doug walked downstairs still tying the bow tie of his tuxedo. It was an instrument of torture. He really should burn the thing. If his uniform hadn't been in his closet in Texas where he lived on base, he'd have worn that.

He smoothed down the front of the jacket, took a deep breath and pushed open the double doors. The place was loud and bright, full of senators, businesspeople and high-ranking military personnel. His father held court at the far end of the room, surrounded by eager ears and fat wallets.

Doug would rather be upstairs with Sabine. They could have watched a ball game or a movie. He could have taken his dad for a round of golf in the morning. He wasn't going to tell the old man that, if it hadn't been for Sabine, Doug probably wouldn't even be here.

People turned to look as he crossed the room. Doug refused champagne from more than one waiter with a silver tray, but, despite his size, what probably struck them was the resemblance between father and son. With his dad being a well-known general, it was a wonder Doug didn't get in more trouble on covert missions. The only difference between them, other than age, was the lighter brown of Doug's skin from his Caucasian mother.

He liked that she was still with him, in that way, but he'd rather have her.

The general looked up as he approached. His father's dark green jacket gleamed with buttons and medals. His face crinkled and laugh lines emerged on his chocolate-colored skin. "Douglas!"

The cigar smoke was strong and made his eyes water. Doug smiled while his dad pounded him on the back. "So where is this mystery woman you chased all the way across the country?"

People around them stopped to look at something.

"She's upstairs resting."

The music also stopped, and the general's bushy white eyebrows rose. "Resting, huh?"

Doug turned around. Sabine was in the doorway, and the room grew still and quiet as people turned to get a look at her in a floor-length dark green dress. Her hair cascaded around her shoulders in a riot of waves and curls. She was beautiful.

The general clapped him on the back. "Does she know she's the one?"

SEVEN

It was too late for second thoughts. Sabine pasted on a smile and crossed the room. The music started up again, and she waved off a waiter's offer of champagne. Rarely did she find herself out of her depth, but she felt it here in a roomful of— *Was that the chairman of the Joint Chiefs of Staff?* Sabine was pretty sure she'd seen him on CNN last week.

With a polite nod she made her way to where Doug stood with a bald older African-American man who was a few inches shorter than Doug, but no less wide. General Richardson was a formidable sight with all those medals pinned to his jacket. Sabine raised her chin as he met her eyes and said something to Doug that she was too far away to hear.

Someone grabbed her arm. Before the threat even fully registered, instinct and training made her react with a spin, ready to strike back at her attacker.

"Whoa, take it easy.... Elena Sanders?"

The name brought with it a rush of memory and emotion, and Sabine lowered her hands. An attack in front of a bunch of armed military servicemen and servicewomen wasn't likely.

She blinked at the man in front of her. "Mr. Adams?"

It had been years since she'd seen anyone from the days when she had trained with the CIA, and here she was, face-to-face with the man who'd given her a fail on her weapons proficiency test. She'd retaken it twice. The years had turned Steve Adams's dark hair to silver at the temples and had deepened the lines around his eyes.

A new wariness was there, emphasized when he scanned the area around them and leaned closer. "What are you doing here? You have a lot of explaining to do."

Sabine made a point to glance at his grip on her arm. There would probably be a bruise tomorrow. When he let her go, she backed up, ready to rip into him for manhandling her for no reason. "It's a party. What do you think I'm doing here?"

Doug stepped up beside her. "Everything okay, Sabine?"

"Sabine?" Steve asked.

She ignored the question. "This is Steve Adams, one of my training officers at the CIA."

Doug shook Steve Adams's hand. The quick tightening around Steve's eyes before Doug let go would have been a wince of pain in anyone else.

"Nice to meet you, Steve."

"I'd like to say it's a pleasure."

Sabine didn't want to feel comfort from the touch of Doug's tuxedo sleeve against her bare arm, but she did. It wouldn't take much for one of them to reach out and take the other's hand.

Focus.

"So, Steve…" Sabine cut through the tension between the two men. "What are you up to these days?"

Steve's eyes flickered again, a trace of confusion he allowed her to see. "I'm a director at Langley now. I have been for the past four years. You?"

"Same old, same old. You know how it goes." She smiled. He would know that she had spent the last few years doing what she did best: gathering intelligence on some of the world's biggest crooks.

"Unfortunately, no, I don't know." Again Steve glanced around the room. He was no doubt as aware as Sabine of the eyes watching them, the ears peeled. "Is there somewhere we can talk in private?"

"I can show you to my father's library."

Sabine trailed behind Doug across the ballroom with Steve beside her. What did this man, a man she at one time considered a mentor, want to talk about? He'd been so surprised to run into her that something strange must be going on. And why did it seem like Doug already knew what Steve was going to tell her? Probably it was CIA business. How had they even known she would be here tonight, at this party? The CIA kept track of its assets, but this was crazy.

Doug opened the door to a room lined with bookshelves. There wasn't a spare space that she could see. It was full, and yet the room didn't feel closed in to her, just warm and open. Sabine would have loved to spend hours in here, lost to worlds of adventure.

The door closed with Doug still in the room. He caught her look and shook his head, like she should've known he would include himself, and turned to Steve. "This room is secure. You don't have to worry about listening devices. You can speak freely."

Steve's eyebrow peaked. "Except that you're here."

If the look on Steve's face was anything to go by, Sabine was going to want Doug to be here for whatever was about to be said. Not that she would tell Steve that Doug was anything more than a regular soldier. "It is okay, Mr. Adams. I trust Sergeant Major Richardson."

Steve's face was blank, a mask of indifference that said enough without saying anything at all. This man felt the need to hide behind nonchalance, which told Sabine of the gravity of the situation.

She chose a dark wood gondola chair that had a green-suede-covered seat. "What is it?"

Steve scanned a bookshelf beside him, then finally came and sat across the cherrywood coffee table in a chair that matched hers. "You have some kind of nerve showing up here, Ms. Sanders. After what you did six years ago, I would think you'd have the good sense to stay away from this part of the country. Either you're incredibly brave or completely reckless."

Doug's mouth opened, and she shot him a look, cutting off whatever he'd been about to say. "I'd love to know what you're talking about, Mr. Adams, but I'm afraid I have no idea. Six years ago, when the Tamaris mission went wrong—"

"Went wrong?" Steve's face flushed. "Three agents, your team, your friends, were all left for dead on that mission. You disappeared. The company spent a considerable amount of time and manpower searching for you to determine if you'd been killed or captured."

"Captured?" Sabine couldn't believe it. "I was left for dead, just like the others. I woke up two days later in a French hospital with three bullet wounds. After I recovered, my new handler told me I had to disappear. He gave me everything I needed to start a new life. It was only after I rebuilt everything from the ground up that I started taking on missions again."

Steve looked her over, as though assessing the truth of her words. "Who is your handler?"

"His name is Neil. That's all I know."

"It would be worth your while to find out more about

him." He paused for a beat. "Ms. Sanders, this situation is very serious. For the past six years, everyone at the CIA has wondered who killed the other members of your team on the Tamaris mission. Some even speculated that you killed them yourself and then disappeared."

"I've given my whole life to the CIA. How can they even say that?"

"Because if what you say is true, then those who speculated that you have gone rogue are, in fact, correct."

"Rogue?"

Steve nodded. "Several times over the last few years, agents out on missions claim to have seen you. There was never any hard evidence to prove it. You're quite adept at that which we trained you for."

"This is the most contrived story I've ever heard." Sabine tamped down the urge to rage at the man before her. Instead she tried to remember the respect she once had for him. "You're saying I was duped into being a rogue agent by someone pretending to be a CIA handler?"

"It's not out of the realm of possibility, if you think about it. They convince you the situation was so bad it was necessary for you to go dark, part of some super-secret department. They provide you with a new identity…*Sabine*. Now you work for them, a fully trained CIA operative at their beck and call. It's clever."

"I am not a pawn. I would know if I wasn't working for the CIA anymore."

Steve didn't seem convinced. "Not if they didn't want you to. Whoever you're working for now convinced you that you're still a CIA agent when you've been number one on our list of rogues since the Tamaris mission. They're evidently very good at what they do."

"This whole thing is crazy."

Doug squeezed her shoulder. "You should listen to him."

She turned her frown on him. "Why? How do you know anything about this?"

"After we saw each other in the Dominican Republic, I gave your information to my commanding officer. He said the same thing. I told you the CIA denied all knowledge of you. They've been looking for you. Though how you managed to change your name and Ben's—and stay hidden this whole time—is beyond me."

"We didn't change Ben's name. I never told the CIA that I had a brother. We went our separate ways for a while after he had graduated from high school, and then he joined the army. We had different last names, anyway, so when I needed a new identity, I borrowed his. It wasn't too hard for the government to find they had accidentally lost a few key records of Ben's. The ones that linked us." She shrugged. "It wasn't anyone else's business but mine that I have—had a half brother."

Sabine looked back at Steve and dread settled over her like a storm cloud. "Are you going to have me arrested?"

He worked his mouth. "You should at least come in to Langley so we can get this whole thing sorted out. There's a lot of stuff to unpack, if we're going to figure out what happened and who this handler of yours is…who he works for."

"Not before I figure out what happened to Ben."

Steve frowned. Sabine filled him in on what had happened since her brother's death and her investigation into who was responsible. She left out the part about her intruder and the exploding hard drive.

Steve sighed. "I understand you want justice for your brother, but the army is no doubt conducting an investigation." Steve looked at Doug, who nodded. "While I'm not unsympathetic to your situation, it's of the utmost importance that you yield yourself to us for questioning. We have to get to the bottom of this."

Sabine strode to the far end of the room and stared at a shelf of historical novels. Her eyes refused to focus on the titles printed on the spines. Her brain was far too full, trying to process what Steve had told her. Could she really be a rogue agent?

She picked through her memories and tried to find some indication that her handler, Neil, was anything other than the CIA agent he had claimed to be. Before seeing Christophe Parelli killed by someone who looked exactly like her, she would have said for certain Neil was who he had said he was. Now she couldn't be sure.

There was just no way to predict the outcome. Sabine could end up in prison, disgraced or most likely the victim of an *accident* that brought about her untimely demise. If she really had been duped into working as an agent against the CIA, then she doubted whoever it was would let her live long enough to provide the actual CIA with enough evidence to discover their identity.

Sabine had been a victim once, long ago. After that she had vowed never to return to such a helpless state. The truth about Ben's death would stay hidden unless she was able to help Doug figure out who had killed her brother and why. There was no way she could turn herself in to the CIA for questioning when they would most likely detain her indefinitely.

She turned back and found both men watching her. "I will help you find out who it is I've been working for."

"Good—"

Sabine cut him off. "But not until after Doug and I find the person who killed my brother. You need to keep this to yourself, Mr. Adams. Do not tell anyone you've seen or spoken to me. In return for your promise, as soon as this is over, I'll turn myself in to the CIA. You can do whatever you want with me."

"Sabine…" Doug's voice was guarded. He was probably right to be worried.

"I'll even work out a meeting with my handler. You can set up surveillance. I'll wear a wire. You can use me however you want to find out who it is I've been working for. But I do what I need to do first."

Steve shook his head. "I don't know about this."

"I don't need you to agree, Mr. Adams. I can walk away right now. I can disappear again, and you'll never find me. I'll still get what I want—time enough to hunt for Ben's killer—while you get nothing."

A thought occurred to her. "If my handler really is working against you, they're no doubt keeping tabs on their asset…me. If they think I've given you anything, they're going to close up shop as fast as possible and go so far underground that you'll never figure it out. It's what I would do."

Doug nodded slowly. "Not before they get rid of all the evidence."

Sabine caught his gaze and knew he'd reached the same conclusion as her. "They'll kill me. Which is not part of my five-year plan."

Steve rubbed a hand down his face. "You want me to pretend I never saw you when a roomful of government staffers just witnessed the two of us meet and leave the room together?"

"There's no reason to believe they'll say anything. Or that they won't. It's a risk, but a calculated one that I can live with. I think I can trust General Richardson's taste in friends."

Doug folded his arms. "You can."

"You want me to sit on this until you decide to turn yourself in? You've been gone for six years as far as anyone at the Agency is concerned." Steve blew out a breath. "You want me to let you leave on good faith?"

"You know me, Mr. Adams. Or at least you did. If what you say is true, I was duped. As far as I'm concerned, I've been nothing but an upright agent of the intelligence community my whole working life. That means, despite being deceived, I'm still as trustworthy as I ever was."

Steve studied her for a moment and then nodded. "Give me some insurance, and I'll trust you."

Sabine snorted. "Typical. You'll trust me, but not without something to hold over me? That's hardly trust, but I don't suppose I expected differently from a CIA agent."

"I could detain you right now."

Doug put himself between her and Steve. "You could try it, but you wouldn't get two feet from my father's house with her."

Steve's eyes widened. "I see. It's like that, is it? You're willing to go to bat for a loose cannon?"

Sabine was as surprised as Steve that Doug put himself between her and the complete destruction of her career and her reputation. Any way she looked at it, this was bad. Was he really willing to jeopardize his life, as well? She stared at Doug's back. In most ways, they were polar opposites. Not to mention that he didn't even trust her. Why was he doing this?

After everything they'd been through, Sabine had come to admire him. She could even admit she was attracted to him, but there was too much grief over Ben between them for anything to develop romantically.

"Being a loose cannon is part of her charm."

Sabine wasn't sure how she felt about that. Was Doug trying to compliment her in a roundabout way? If she was a loose cannon, he was about as impulsive as a piece of plywood. Talk about opposites attracting.

Steve looked around Doug. His eyes zeroed in on her. "You have one week."

"A week!"

"That's all I'm giving you. Seven days from now I expect to get a call from the security guards at Langley asking if I'll authorize your admittance."

Sabine nodded. That was the best offer she was likely to get. "Done."

She reached up and clasped the flower on her necklace, one of the last gifts she'd received from Ben. A peace offering for the way he had blown up after he'd found out she was a CIA agent. Now that might not even be true.

"You have something to give me?"

Sabine found a notepad and pen in the top drawer of the desk, scribbled on it, tore off the page and handed it to Steve. "I'll see you in a week."

Steve Adams pocketed the paper and closed the library door behind him.

She turned to Doug. "You didn't seem too surprised about what Steve had to say. You want to tell me what you knew about all this?"

"You want to tell me what was on that piece of paper?"

"No."

Doug smiled, completely disarming her. "Good, because I'd rather dance with you anyway."

"But—"

"Sabine." He came around the desk to her. "Let's go back to the party. We both need time to let this settle in."

"But—"

He lifted her hand to his mouth and kissed the back of it. "Have I told you how beautiful you are in this dress?"

EIGHT

Doug held his arms loose, when everything in him wanted to clasp Sabine to him as tight as possible as they swayed slowly in the middle of the dance floor. Couples all around them moved to the rhythm of an old love song, caught up in the moment.

The comment his dad had made when she entered the ballroom ran through his mind. Was she the one? He could hardly see there being a time in either of their lives when they might be free to begin a relationship. No matter how appealing the thought was.

And yet it felt so natural to hold her in his arms. He wanted to keep her there as long as possible, but circumstances seemed to conspire against them. A cloud of foreboding settled on him—like if he let her go he'd lose something he would never get back.

Doug wanted to go to Langley with her when she turned herself in. He wanted to be her line of defense. Mostly he wanted to stick with her and see where this might lead, and there was little time to lose if they wanted to find out what had happened to Ben.

But Sabine was wound so tight, she needed to take her mind off what was going on.

He was still floored by everything he'd learned about

her from Adams. The CIA guy had been genuinely surprised to see her. When Adams had said she'd been AWOL for the past six years, Doug had discovered why. Watching her process the news that she'd been so thoroughly deceived into being a rogue agent and then come up with a solid plan that Adams had agreed with had been impressive, to say the least.

Doug had a huge amount of respect for the woman in his arms. She possessed strength few people would even be able to understand. Even so, there was hardness in her that he didn't know if he'd ever be able to penetrate, no matter how close they grew. There was little that was soft and sweet about her, despite how good at dancing she was.

"You're a great dancer," Sabine said.

Doug chuckled.

She tipped her head back. "What?"

"I was just thinking the same about you."

"Oh…well." She glanced around everywhere but at him. "This is a wonderful room."

Warmth moved through him, and his stomach unclenched. "It is. My mom and dad used to dance in here late at night when they were all alone. They'd put a record on, dim the lights. I would sneak in past curfew, and they'd be in here, totally oblivious to anything except each other. It was kind of frustrating. And also gross to a teenage boy."

Sabine laughed and then seemed to realize they had stopped dancing, and yet he still held her.

"You should do that more often."

"What?"

"Laugh like that. It's a pretty sound."

"Thank you. You're sweet."

Doug rolled his eyes. "I don't think I've ever been called sweet before."

"It's true."

"Do me a favor and don't tell anyone, okay? I've got a reputation to maintain."

Sabine looked at the floor and then back up at him, her eyes a shade darker. "I'm scared."

"I couldn't tell."

"That's because I'm good at my job. Which is probably what got me in this mess in the first place."

"Sabine—" He was going to tell her to leave all the worry for tomorrow, but she cut him off.

"You are sweet." Her eyes held his.

Doug shifted his weight.

"You loved seeing your mom and dad dance."

"Yeah, I did. I loved how in love they were, but they also made it clear I was a part of what was between them, so I didn't mind too much when it felt like I was overlooked. When my mom was diagnosed, it was like the light went out of my dad's eyes. He kept it together for her, though. Then she died, and he threw himself into his work like never before. I left for basic training, and when I came back it wasn't to the father I'd known. He was never the same after she died."

"Is that why you let your fiancée break up with you? You wanted the same thing your parents had, and you knew it wasn't her."

"You're saying I let Tara walk away because I was just biding my time with her?" Doug didn't know whether to be offended at her presumption or impressed at how astute she was. "I've always assumed no woman would be able to handle the stress of my job, but I probably did hold myself back. After Tara broke our engagement, it was easier to date women who were just friends, or friends of friends. Romantic feelings make things more complicated."

"I agree with you."

"That doesn't mean I don't dream of having what my

mom and dad had. Someone to share my home with, to have children with and to see the kind of people they grow up to be."

"I thought that once." She shrugged her slender shoulders. "What little girl doesn't dream of happily ever after with her handsome prince? But life isn't like that. Perfect relationships are the stuff of fiction."

"So you just stopped dreaming?" He studied her. What had happened to her and Ben? "What made you so hard?"

She stepped out of his arms. "When you witness something as horrific as what Ben and I were forced to endure, it changes you."

Doug took her hand and wove them through the crowd to the open French doors that led to the patio. At the stone ledge he turned and laid his hands on her shoulders. "Tell me what happened."

Sabine took a deep breath. "You're going to regret asking me that."

"I don't think so." She was fighting tears. "I need you to trust me. This secret of yours is tearing you up. No matter how badly you refuse to believe that, I can see it in your eyes."

She turned away to look out across the manicured lawn. "I was nine, and Ben was five the day my mom shot my dad."

"You can't be—"

"You asked." Her chest heaved. "If you want to know so badly, then be quiet while I tell you."

Doug closed his mouth.

"He was actually my stepdad. Ben's dad. He was good to both of us, and I loved him. We were playing cards, when Mom walked in with this look on her face."

Sabine wrapped her arms around her waist. "She had a gun. I pulled Ben across the room as far away as I could.

She yelled for us to stop. Said something to Dad about betrayal and then shot him. There was so much blood. When she turned to us, she still had that look on her face. She said, 'I should have done this a long time ago' and pointed the gun at me and Ben. We ran out the back door and through this gap in the fence while she shot at us. We just kept running until we couldn't run anymore."

She took another deep breath. "Some cops found us in an alley behind a Dumpster a couple of miles away. I remember the smell and how freezing it was. I've hated cold places ever since."

"Your mom is in prison?"

Sabine shook her head. "They never caught her."

"What?"

"She got away. No one has seen her since. I guess disappearing runs in the family, because I seem to have the knack for it, too."

"You're nothing like her."

"You don't know that, Doug. I'm good at my job. So good everyone at the CIA apparently thinks I killed my whole team six years ago. Maybe I'm more like her than I want to admit."

"I don't believe that." He took a chance, reached out and touched her cheek, thumbed away a tear. "Thank you for telling me. You took a chance trusting me, and I won't let you down."

She smiled a sweet, sad smile. One that brought him closer, made him want to express his gratitude that she had shared her darkest moment with him. He leaned in and—

"There you are."

Sabine stepped back. Her face was probably beet red, since they'd been seconds away from what promised to be a memorable encounter. At least it would have been, if the look in Doug's eyes was anything to go by.

The general stood in the doorway with a wide smile on his face, like he knew exactly what they'd been about to do. "I was wondering where you two got to."

Doug grabbed her hand and pulled her back to his side. She sucked in a breath and tried not to look as guilty as she felt. Their almost-kiss wasn't something she would ever regret, but getting caught by his dad made her feel like she was acting out against that dream parent she used to wish for.

She'd long ago given up on the childhood fantasy of having good, healthy parents. Real life was much harder. There was little space left over for wishes. When she looked at Doug, it was like the petals of a flower unfolding to the summer sun. The man beside her made her want to dream again.

Sabine refocused. They were both waiting for her to say something. "I'm sorry, what?"

They laughed, though Doug's laughter sounded more embarrassed. When she looked at him, she realized he was as nervous as she was.

The general stepped forward. "I asked if you wanted to dance, my dear. It would be my great honor to spend time with the woman my son brought home. I thought you might indulge me, being as it is my birthday."

Sabine couldn't help but accept. "Certainly, General. I would love to."

He held out his arm. "Please, call me Andrew."

He led her to the dance floor where the crowd had thinned out, leaving only the late-night die-hard partiers. Wrung out, she tried not to lean too heavily on Andrew… until he shifted closer to her and absorbed the bulk of her weight.

"I won't keep you long."

He knew.

"My son should have better sense than keeping you up when you're exhausted."

"I appreciate your concern, Gen—Andrew. The past few weeks have been some of the hardest of my life, and your son has been an invaluable help. I can see where he gets it. You should be very proud."

"Thank you. I am." Andrew frowned. "I'm selfish enough to admit I would have liked to see him ascend through the ranks and follow more in the way my career progressed, but Doug has always made his own way in life. I encouraged that."

"I know he's Spec Op—"

"He's a clerk, dear."

Sabine blinked. A clerk?

"That's how we refer to it. The men of their field like to keep their occupation on the 'down low,' as the kids like to say."

"Of course." Sabine smiled. "You know my brother worked with Doug?"

Andrew nodded. "I'm very sorry for your loss."

"Thank you. Even though his duties as a…clerk kept him busy, my brother was still a huge part of my life. I miss him."

The general nodded. His eyes were shadowed with the same grief she felt. Then he seemed to shake it off, and pulled her into an elaborate turn that took her breath away and made her laugh.

"May I ask how you've managed to keep going, since you also suffered grief in your life?" Maybe she was being too forward, but Sabine hoped he would answer.

"That I have. Many men under my command, as well as my wife, Doug's mother."

Sabine nodded. "He told me."

The general smiled, small and wistful. "She was a gem of a woman. Much like you."

"How do you go on?"

"Have I? I'm not sure I've really moved on from that day. It seems to have stayed with me and not a day goes by that I don't remember. That's what happens when you lose a part of your heart. After that, you just do the best you can with the bit you have left."

Sabine wanted to cry for him but held the rush of emotion back. He wouldn't want her pity. "Was it worth it? I mean, if you knew how it was going to end, would you still let yourself fall for her?"

The general's arms fell to his sides. Sabine was about to apologize when he spoke. "Yes. Absolutely, unequivocally yes. Even for the simple fact of having Doug with me still. It is hard to lose the person you were supposed to grow old with, but you cherish what time you have together. No one knows the future, Elena. So you live life to the fullest. You take the risk. Because if you don't, how do you know you're really alive?"

The general kissed her cheek and walked away.

It was tempting to want to live life to the fullest. She wouldn't be able to hold back anymore. If she wanted a relationship between her and Doug to be worth anything at all, then she'd have to give it everything she had. But a man like Doug would never accept a strong woman inclined to take care of herself. He'd want to be the hero.

She wanted a man who would be her equal partner in life. Someone to stand beside her, instead of in front trying to protect her from things she had plenty of experience with. If she hadn't learned how to take care of herself by now, she wouldn't have the job she loved so much.

Doug no doubt wanted a woman who was the stay-at-home type. His wife would be with their kids while he went all over the world on missions. Missions he couldn't tell her about. At one time Sabine had dreamed of a real family that was all her own, but life had stolen those dreams. Still, it was a tempting thought, if only to see how different it might be from Maxwell's coldness.

The memory of her ex-husband crested over her like a wave of ice water. It wasn't worth going there, even in comparison. That time in her life was over. He had a new wife now, one he was free to ignore unless he was in the mood to criticize everything about her.

She would have liked to think she was strong enough to fight the past and go for it with Doug. But if it didn't work, it would destroy her. Could she take the risk?

Considering her abysmal history, staying alone was a whole lot simpler. She should probably look into getting a cat or something. Cats were friendly, right?

Then Sabine realized something else.

The general had called her Elena.

Doug sipped his drink and watched Sabine leave the ballroom. He could see how tired she was; she hadn't really needed to make her excuses to him. On the way out, she said something to his father that made the old man smile.

"Sergeant Major."

Doug turned and came face-to-face with his boss's boss's boss's… He lost track after a while. "Major General, sir."

They shook hands. Major General Robert Taylor was his father's golf buddy and also bore a striking resemblance to Bruce Willis. Doug would have saluted, but they were both out of uniform, and this was the room he used to slide around in his socks with his friends after they ate too much candy.

"I read your report."

Doug could see the major general didn't believe Sabine's theory about being set up for Parelli's death. "Any idea what the repercussions will be?"

"Depends. The army certainly has no problem that a weapons dealer is dead. Outside of us, things get more complicated."

Doug snorted. "That's a fact. Why do you think I'm content being a noncommissioned officer?"

"It does create a certain distance between you and all the bureaucracy, doesn't it?" The major general's eyes gleamed. "Good move. Wish I'd had the same foresight as you."

"Feeling the pressure of command?"

The major general huffed. "Nothing I can't handle."

"Of course." Something hard emerged in the older man's eyes, and Doug wasn't sure he would like where the conversation was about to go.

"Word to the wise, son. This girl could spell big trouble for you. I'm not sure you want to get tangled up where she's heading. Could be the end of your career. Just a little friendly advice, since you've been like a nephew to me for a long time, Doug. Women like that are never good for us." The old man laughed. "Trust me. I've been married three times. All of them were strong…you could even say dangerous women. I know it feels exciting and new right now, but if you let yourself get sucked in, when she walks away—which she will—there won't be much of you that she leaves behind."

"I appreciate the warning, sir."

"But you're not going to listen to me. No, don't argue. I can see it in your eyes, kid. Take it or leave it. When this girl's troubles all descend on her, you won't want to be in the middle of it."

The major general sucked down the remnants of his drink and left.

Did he really believe Sabine would do that? Her job was the kind that forced her to give it all and rarely let anyone else walk away with anything to show for it—aside from bruises. She could absolutely take care of herself. Fiercely independent, that's what she was. Or was it that life had taught her to guard her heart above all else to keep from risking it being broken…again? It would take a lot to get through that shell of hers.

Could she let someone in enough to be comfortable including them in her inner circle? Ben had lived there. Now that Doug knew what the two of them had been through, he could see how saving her little brother's life meant that they stuck with each other from then on.

Would she ever let Doug in like that?

NINE

"Richardson." Doug rubbed the sleep from his eyes and listened to the voice bark instructions through the phone. "Understood."

He pushed away the urge to mourn for what would have been his first full night of sleep in days and got up. It was 4:00 a.m. After he splashed cold water on his face, Doug put the few things he'd got out of his duffel back in and zipped it closed.

He tapped on Sabine's door and waited, but she didn't appear. Sleeping that deeply wasn't good in her line of work. At the same time he was glad she felt safe enough at his dad's house to get the rest she needed. He peered in to check on her.

The bed was empty.

The sheets and blanket were rumpled like they'd gotten twisted up while she had tossed around trying to fall asleep. He didn't want to be going on a mission when she was like this, but it couldn't be helped. Work called. He'd have to trust her to stay here and wait.

The Raven, or someone who worked for him—or her, he supposed, since they had no idea—had withdrawn money from a bank in the Cayman Islands. The team was off on a treasure hunt that could lead who-knew-where. He'd get the full details at the briefing, which would likely happen on the plane since the team was spread all over the place.

Downtime was a bit of a misnomer when you were still effectively "on call." That was the nature of his work, and he wouldn't have it any other way. Being a nine-to-five with weekends off had never been his thing.

Sabine's bathroom was empty. The major general's words came back to Doug, and he had to push away the distrust. Just because she wasn't where he could find her didn't mean she had betrayed him. She was Ben's sister. That fact alone was enough for him to know he could trust her. Ben would never have spoken so highly of her if she was their enemy. Sure, she'd been deceived into working for someone other than the CIA. That didn't mean she was working against the U.S. It wasn't like she was an agent for the Raven.

Sabine wasn't in the kitchen, TV room or the library. A low light shone from under the door to his dad's office, so he went in to ask the general if he knew where Sabine was.

Sabine's fingers froze on the keyboard. Doug was in the doorway, and his mouth hung open. She slid the chair back from the computer. "It's not what you think."

He folded his arms across his chest. "Is that right?"

She wasn't going to be able to talk her way out of this. If she did, it would destroy the small bit of progress they had made toward trusting each other. "I was looking for something."

"There are a lot of things to find in here. You know, I was just thinking to myself, no, there's no way Sabine would ever betray me because Ben trusted her. I guess you deceived him, too."

She gasped.

"Good thing all the sensitive information is secured."

He thought she was capable of that? She would never, ever have betrayed her brother. "Is that your way of warning me away from betraying the very country I've been working for this whole time? You think I'm some kind of spy against America?"

Except that was exactly what people thought of her.

He crossed the room. "You have to admit it looks pretty suspicious. Charm the general's son. Blow up a hard drive so I have no choice but to bring you to the safest place I know, the general's own house. Break into his office in the middle of the night to steal secrets."

"You forget that your dead teammate was my little brother, whose killer I will find."

"By breaking in here?"

"The door was unlocked."

"Sabine."

"Your dad called me *Elena,* okay?"

Surprise flickered on his face before he quashed it.

She blew out a breath. "I need to know what he knows. If there's information going around about me, I have to know what it says. I'm so twisted around, worried about what's going to happen to me."

His lips thinned. "Most people would just say, 'Hey, General, why'd you call me that?'"

"I guess I'm not most people."

"I guess not." He sighed. "Did you find anything?"

"You want to know what dirty secrets I'm privy to?" She narrowed her eyes. "Sorry, but I didn't get through the security features on his computer yet." He smirked, which she took as a challenge. "Come back in ten minutes, then I'll tell you something juicy."

"Not going to happen." He studied her. "You couldn't have come to me? You felt you had to sneak in here—"

"I couldn't sleep. It seemed like a good time, and I didn't

want to wake you." She closed her eyes. "I don't know why I feel like I have to justify myself to you."

"And yet you'll betray our trust because you couldn't tell us the truth?"

She stood up, to put them on more level ground instead of having him tower over her. "Would you have?"

"What have I said or done that gave you the feeling you couldn't trust me?"

"That's not what this is about." Besides, his whole job was secrets. Why hadn't she seen that before? This could never work. There was no way they'd ever be able to completely trust each other, forever wondering if the other one was holding out.

His eyes darkened. "As much as I'd love to stay and work this out with you, Sabine, I have to go."

"You're leaving?" She walked around the desk. She needed to get by him with a sliver of her self-respect still intact. "I guess I should have known better, should never have told you about my parents. Ben never did. Maybe he was right not to trust you with it."

He grabbed her arm as she passed.

She looked at him but didn't let the look of pain on his face penetrate her mask. "Time will tell."

"What's that supposed to mean? Sabine, I got a call. The team moves out first thing this morning. I have to go. It's my job."

"Ah, yes, the almighty job. Greatest above all things."

"Sabine—"

She shook her head. "Maybe I can trust you, maybe not. Maybe I'm the bad guy. I guess we'll see, since I'm obviously stupid enough to stick around right under the noses of everyone who wants me out of commission, just to find out. Boy, do I wish attraction didn't make me an idiot."

He caught up to her at the door. "You seriously like me?"

"That's not what I meant." At least, she didn't want it to be. She wanted to forget she'd said it. Why had that slipped out? She had to change the subject. "How long will you be gone? You know, so I can be waiting by the phone."

He sighed. "Honestly? I have no idea. I could be a day or it could be weeks."

"Weeks?"

"You know how it is, Sabine."

She did. Ben's schedule of being overseas versus being in the States had been erratic to say the least. "I'll be sure to stay here like a good girl and wait for the big, strong man to come home."

He sighed. "Just promise me you won't disappear. Or do anything dangerous."

She didn't want it to affect her, but it did. "I don't invite these things, you know. And I don't like being a victim."

"When I look at you, a victim is the last thing I see."

Sabine was floored, but managed to keep her jaw from dropping. A few more of those petals opened to the sun.

"This house is safe for you. My dad and I aren't hiding anything."

"You can't believe that. Not when you both have enough secrets to fill the Library of Congress."

"I promise you, Sabine, we aren't hiding anything that could harm you. We're trying to help you, and I need you to let me do that."

She studied his face. "Okay, I believe you."

"Will you promise me something else?"

She nodded.

"Don't do anything to hurt my dad."

"I would never—"

He sighed. "Just say you won't, so I can believe you and trust you while I'm gone."

It grated that he felt he had to make her promise not to

hurt his dad. As if she really would. But since he'd found her searching his dad's computer, she relented. "I promise."

As he walked away, Sabine realized he took a little piece of her heart with him. She watched from the office as the general appeared at the bottom of the stairs in blue-and-white striped pajamas and a pair of slippers. Doug hugged his dad and looked back at her, but she didn't know what that look meant.

Then he was gone.

Andrew turned and saw her in the doorway to his office. His eyes widened. "Find anything interesting?"

Her cheeks heated, and she knew that—even in the dim light of predawn—he saw her embarrassment.

"Come." He waved toward the kitchen. "We can have tea, and you can tell me. I doubt either of us is going to sleep any more tonight."

The light above the stove was already on when they entered, the curtains pulled tight across the window. The effect was privacy and a sense of detachment from the outside world that helped her forget what was going on. Even if it was fleeting, it was still nice.

Sabine sat at the table while Andrew filled the kettle. He turned back, folded his arms across his chest and gave her a look she'd seen on Doug's face several times. She looked at the table's surface. The refrigerator hummed. Deeply ingrained traits that had been cemented by her CIA training gave her a sick feeling in her stomach. But with any luck, if she trusted him, he'd reciprocate and tell her why he'd called her Elena.

She sucked in a deep breath, pushed away the discomfort of opening up and launched into the whole story of her parents, the CIA, Ben's death and how she met Doug. The general smiled when she told him how she'd ditched

Doug in the café and how he'd come after her in Seattle, bursting into her house to save her.

"Sounds like the two of you have been good for each other."

"I'm not sure Doug sees it that way."

Andrew's wrinkled face brightened. "I think he needs someone exactly like you, Sabine. You're a firecracker."

She laughed. "Was that even a compliment?"

"Honey, it's the highest one I know. Doug's mama was a firecracker. There was never a dull moment with that woman." His gaze took on a wistful air.

"I'm not sure we'll ever get to that place. There's a lot that could go wrong if we're not careful."

He squeezed her fingers. "If there was nothing to overcome, how would you know it was worth fighting for? You have to ask yourself if he's worth it."

"I suppose you're going to tell me that he is. After all, he's your son."

Andrew shook his head. "My opinion shouldn't play into it. You're the only one who can answer the questions of your heart."

Sabine was quiet for a moment. "Thank you."

"You're wondering why I called you Elena last night."

"Yes."

"A lot of paperwork has crossed my desk in the last week. Mission reports and the like. It was nothing but an old man's slip of the tongue." He studied her. "Do you wish to be called that, or should we stick with your cover, *Sabine?*"

The name Elena brought back a lot of memories of her mother and stepfather, of years spent in the fight to survive foster care. Then again, she had been accepted into the CIA under her real name—Elena Sanders.

"I prefer Sabine." She smiled. "Sabine is the firecracker."

Andrew laughed.

"Elena wasn't nearly so tough, even if she did make it through CIA training. She feels like who I used to be, while Sabine is who I am now." She remembered Doug's parting words. "She's a survivor."

"I have to ask. You changed your name and used Ben's last name?"

"I had covered my tracks well enough that it seemed to be okay and for him to have a room there, being as the house was under my cover name and he wasn't listed on anything. He needed a home base when he wasn't working, and it'd been long enough that my new identity was established, but some part of me still can't help thinking maybe someone found me—or Ben discovered something—and that's what got him killed."

"He was killed on a mission."

"I know that."

"You still worry it had something to do with the job you chose?" Andrew shook his head. Behind him, the kettle had begun to boil. "Trust my son."

"I do."

"If Doug thought Ben's death was because of you and not the Raven, he would have told you."

"The Raven?"

"The reason your brother was killed. Doug's team found evidence that links the Raven to the man who funded the hired gun."

"Christophe Parelli."

Andrew nodded.

"So Parelli hired the guy who killed Ben, but Parelli really worked for this Raven guy?"

"That's as much as I know."

"And now Parelli's dead, too."

The kettle began to whistle. Andrew stood to make the tea.

There was a crack, like breaking glass, and the curtain billowed up as something flew in the window. Shards of glass sprayed the room, and Sabine didn't have time to react. The projectile dented the fridge and hit the floor. Andrew grabbed his chest.

Before she could reach him, he fell.

TEN

Sabine had to fight not to roll her eyes at the cop. "No, I don't know who could have done this. Or why. How many times do I have to say it?"

"Until I'm satisfied, I'm afraid."

She bit back a retort and adjusted her perch on the rock-solid hospital waiting-room chair. The police detective's eyes had dark circles that overshadowed the fine lines on his face. After she adjusted her estimate of his age for the fact that he had a tough job, Sabine still guessed somewhere over fifty. Bald with a soft middle, he looked more mobster than cop.

"I know you're tired, Ms. Surleski, and I appreciate your answering these questions. It's important we get to the bottom of…"

Doug pushed through the doors at the end of the hall.

"Ms. Surleski—"

She ignored the cop, already out of her chair, and ran toward Doug. She wanted a hug. The force of the need to be held made her stop short. Why was the instinct to seek him out for comfort so strong? Doug must have seen the look on her face, the war between what she wanted and what was appropriate. He shook his head and gathered her in his arms.

Sabine sighed, not wanting to think too much about how nice it felt to be surrounded by his warmth. "I can't believe you're here."

"I hadn't left yet. My colonel gave me permission to come, and the team went without me, but—" He shook his head. "Let's just say they'll be fine. Not sure how I feel about being expendable, though."

Sabine nodded, thankful beyond words that he was here. That she could support him. "I'm still waiting for word."

"Uh, excuse me. Ms. Surleski?"

Sabine ignored the look on Doug's face at the mention of the name she used on missions. The use of that identity was risky, but she was too tired and too overwhelmed with worry about Andrew to figure out which was safer—the name of the woman who killed Christophe Parelli or the name she usually went by.

The one the CIA now knew.

She turned back to the cop. "This is General Richardson's son."

"Of course." The two men shook hands, and the detective turned to her. "If we can continue with our questions?"

She nodded and they walked back. Doug sat beside her.

"You said a rock flew through the window?"

"That's right."

"And that led to the heart attack?"

Doug flinched, but she ignored it. Instead she tried to smile and hoped it looked pleasant.

She hadn't planned on mentioning the note attached to the rock. Not that she wanted to lie to the police. She'd just spent too many years taking care of her own problems. The police, the Feds, whoever got their hands on the note to test it for fingerprints or whatever wouldn't have the first clue what it meant. Plus Doug would want to see it, anyway. Plenty of reasons to slip it in her pocket.

TREAD CAREFULLY.

Sabine couldn't have said how she knew, but it was meant for her, and it was about their investigation into Ben's death. It was a waste of ink as far as she was concerned. Nothing was going to stop her from finding out who had killed her brother.

The detective sipped his coffee. Rude, since she didn't have anything to drink and he hadn't offered. She could dearly use some caffeine. The adrenaline surge from seeing Andrew fall down had long since worn off, and she was still waiting for news about his condition.

"You have no idea who could have done this?"

"No, I have no idea. Just like I told everyone else who has interviewed me since I got here. All I want is to find out if Andrew is okay. Not sit here answering questions from everyone who thinks this is their business to investigate."

Doug shot her a look, his eyebrow raised, but she wasn't going to back down.

Apparently when a high-ranking military official was attacked at home, everyone wanted to know what the deal was. This cop was the fourth person to interview her in the last two hours.

Every agency in existence had been through the waiting room where she sat—the FBI, the Secret Service, federal agents with the military. She'd seen less people in the center of London on a Saturday night.

Still Sabine was impressed by the attention the general was getting. Most likely it was the result of how much respect he'd earned and how many friends he'd made over the years. Friends who cared enough to move heaven and earth to make sure he was okay.

That was why she humored them all by answering their questions. Not too long ago Sabine would have taken off the minute Andrew was in the hands of EMTs. Tonight she had stuck around. Maybe because, even though they had only met the day before, Andrew meant a lot to her. Maybe it was the shared connection they had in Doug. Either way she wanted him to know she was here for him.

The detective didn't look too impressed. In fact he looked downright insulted. "This is clearly the jurisdiction of local police."

Sabine stood. "Look, I've answered your questions, but I will not be dragged into a tug-of-war between you and the FBI and everyone else. If you'll excuse me, I'm going to get an update on the general's status."

She crossed to the desk where a nurse sat. The young woman had pink hair and a bored expression on her face. "Help you?"

"I'd like an update on General Richardson. It's been two hours, and no one's told me anything."

The nurse sniffed.

Sabine realized her tone could have been nicer but, under the circumstances, couldn't bring herself to feel guilty.

"Are you a relative?"

"I am." Doug appeared beside her. "His son."

The double doors at the end of the waiting room swished open. A good-looking middle-aged man in a white coat came in, talking with the general's housekeeper. Jean's sleek hair was disheveled, and she grasped a balled-up tissue in one hand.

Sabine rushed over. "What is it? Andrew's okay, right?"

Jean sucked in a shaky breath, and the doctor turned to Doug, probably seeing the resemblance between father and son. "The general had a heart attack. He's stable now, but we'll be keeping him here and running tests later today, after he's had a chance to rest."

Jean motioned to Sabine, and they stepped aside while Doug asked the doctor questions.

"Will I be able to see him?" Sabine asked.

Jean's eyes hardened. "I don't think that's a good idea. It's been a long night and Andrew is sleeping. Besides, Doug is here now."

"Oh…of course."

Sabine tried not to be disappointed that they'd left her out in the waiting room tied up being interviewed until the general was asleep and she couldn't see him. "I'll stay until he wakes up then."

Jean smiled but it didn't reach her eyes. "That's really not necessary. Don't feel like you have to stick around."

"I don't really have anywhere else to go." She was supposed to be under the radar. Where better than a hospital full of staff…and security guards? She'd promised Doug she would stay safe, though. And she wanted to be near him.

"I'm sure you'll think of something."

Sabine flinched. She turned too fast and nearly stumbled, but held herself together long enough to get to the hall with some kind of dignity. It had been a long time since she'd been dismissed so thoroughly. To her surprise, it stung in a way she hadn't felt since Maxwell's infidelity had come to light.

More than that, it hurt to realize the pain was so familiar. It had stuck with her all this time without her knowledge.

In a lot of ways the divorce had been a relief. After all the stress and pain of dividing one life back into two she had resolved not to enter into another relationship that left her vulnerable. Now she was free to live. She'd been happy, on her own terms.

Or so she thought.

Sabine swiped a tear from her cheek and pushed away the old feeling of inadequacy. She just wasn't the kind of person who inspired love in other people.

After her mom killed Ben's dad and tried to kill them she'd resolved with a child's understanding that there was something missing in her. Ben's love had filled a lot of the gaps and helped her to heal a great deal—both before and after the disaster that was her marriage to Maxwell. But despite Ben's acceptance of her, that old feeling somehow never went away.

A young woman stepped out of a side room and almost collided with her. Sabine offered a quick apology. The girl's face was the picture of peace, though her eyes were red and puffy like she'd been crying. She smiled and stepped past Sabine, who looked up at the door. It was the hospital's chapel.

Crying in a hospital could mean anything—a loved one in an accident or suffering a terminal illness. Maybe the crying girl had recently lost someone close to her, or she could be worrying about a friend. And yet the look on her face had been radiant.

Ben had looked the same way the last time Sabine had seen him. When she had asked him what was different, she got a wide smile for an answer. He'd said Doug had "led him to the Lord," whatever that meant. Ben had become a Christian, but she didn't really understand it.

What good had it done her brother, anyway? He'd found religion and it got him killed. In reality that probably wasn't what happened, but she couldn't ignore the timing. Within two weeks of becoming a Christian, Ben was dead. Not exactly a good advertisement.

Her phone buzzed. She drew it from her pocket and

looked around to make sure she wasn't going to get in trouble for using her cell in a hospital.

We need to meet.

Her body tensed, readied for battle. Not with the enemy, but with her own handler.

This was her first contact with Neil since she'd found out that he had lied about her working for the CIA the past six years. If she was going to get to the bottom of things, she had to meet with him…and play things very carefully.

She sent a text back.

Where and when?

Doug hadn't been in a hospital since his mom had died.

His dad lay wrapped in a white blanket, asleep to the steady beep of machines. Doug decided he wasn't going to lose another parent to illness. He laid his hand on his dad's weathered one, and the old man's eyes flickered open.

"I wasn't sleeping. I was just resting my eyes."

"Sleep is good, Dad." The last thing Doug wanted was for him to downplay all this and wind up hurt worse.

"I'll rest if you go to your girl. Sabine needs you more than I do right now."

"I know."

"And what are you going to do, anyway? Just stand there all night staring at me?"

Doug snorted. He put his hand on the old man's head, leaned down and touched his forehead to it. "I'll be back tomorrow."

The general shifted and dislodged the blanket. "Not if you have better things to do, you won't."

Doug would come back the next day. Nothing would

be going on that was more important than checking on his dad. He reached down and straightened the blankets. "We'll see."

It wouldn't do to have the old man think he meant to come and visit no matter what. The dance of their relationship was a delicate one, despite the manner in which they spoke to each other. He couldn't let on how much he needed his dad. Nor would his dad ever let on how much he wanted Doug there.

His mom was the one who had brought the two of them together. Would there ever be a day when they could just say what they meant? Doug looked back at his dad lying in the bed, and his heart squeezed. His mom had gone into the hospital and had never come out. A heart attack was a far cry from terminal pancreatic cancer, but, to Doug's little-boy heart, it felt the same.

Lord, don't let my dad die.

He turned away from the sight of the slow rise and fall of his dad's chest, then walked until the door closed on the beeping.

Out in the waiting room Jean paced, wringing her fingers together.

"Hey, you okay?"

She shook her head, tears in her eyes.

"What is it? Where's Sabine?"

"I'm so sorry, Doug. I was really mean to her. And after she did so much to help Andrew. She was right there. She even got him an aspirin before the paramedics arrived. Probably saved his life. I'm afraid it was my fault."

She needed to finish her story so he could go to Sabine. "What happened?"

"I was just so mad. I only found out what happened when the hospital called to say Andrew was asking for me. I thought your Sabine purposely didn't tell me. I froze her out. Then when she walked away I saw the look on her face. She was just trying to be here for us and be supportive. I feel so guilty."

Doug tried to muster up some sympathy, but he was exhausted. It was almost dawn. He had no doubt Sabine really was hurt when Jean rebuffed her. "Jean—"

"I know, I know, but I can't apologize because she hasn't come back in."

"I'll find her. I'll tell her you're sorry."

"Please, Doug."

He took a step back, ready to alert hospital security to start a search for Sabine. "I'll find her."

He headed for the elevator. There was no reason to suspect Sabine was in immediate danger, but something about her being alone—even in a busy hospital—put him on alert. Add to that her being upset and he figured he better find her fast. His finger hammered the down button, and he had to remind himself yet again that she was a trained CIA agent who was absolutely capable of taking care of herself. Now he just had to convince his heart not to worry about her.

Was this their future, constantly fretting about each other's well-being?

If that was the case, Doug wasn't so fired up to let things between him and Ben's sister get any deeper than they already were. Doug really didn't know what kind of woman she was. They'd had limited contact before Ben's death, only small talk at team barbecues when everyone brought their families. Because Doug hadn't let it be more.

Now they were thrown in this situation together and struggling to figure out each other plus what was going on.

He got off the elevator on the first floor and made for the front entrance. He didn't know why he was going outside, only that the instinct of flight usually made people head for the nearest exit.

Sure enough, she was at the curb about to get in a taxi.

"Sabine." He ran to catch up. "Where are you going?"

She straightened and stood in the gap between the open cab door and the body of the car. "I have to go."

"I know what Jean said. She's sorry. She was upset about my dad and she didn't mean to freeze you out." He touched her elbow. "I thought you would go and see my dad with me."

She shook her head, and he didn't like the lack of emotion on her face. "I didn't want to get in the middle of a family thing. You needed time with him."

"No, I needed a buffer against the fear that was about to drown me seeing him lying there just like my mom." Doug's throat hitched. He hadn't meant to say that much, to lay the weight of it on her. He prayed she wouldn't get scared away. "Don't go."

"I have a meeting, Doug. There's too much that needs to be resolved."

So that's what it was. Sabine had switched to work mode. "What happened? Did your handler contact you?"

She nodded. "I have to find out if the last six years were a lie."

"Let me help you. If we can get an ID on your handler, we'll know more about who we're dealing with."

"I have to know who wanted me out of the CIA and why that woman looked like me." She bit her lip and looked down.

"What is it?"

Her eyes lifted. "Will you come with me? I know it's a lot to ask with your dad and all, but—"

"Wouldn't miss it."

However much he had tried to convince himself that

things were still developing between them, the fact was that he was already in deep with this woman. He'd been attracted for a long time. His heart just saw the woman, not the problems that could emerge.

Especially when she found out Ben's death was his fault.

ELEVEN

"Remember to breathe. This is just like any other meeting you've had with your handler."

Sabine tucked the listening device in her ear. "I have done this before, you know. I'm aware of the procedure and the risks."

Doug had parked in a crowded lot at the mall in Boise. It had been a long plane flight, considering they'd gone from Seattle to D.C. only the day before. She'd never flown so much in such a short space of time. If only she could have done it using her real ID, then she could use all these Air Miles she was earning. A vacation sounded good.

His hand rested on her shoulder and jolted her from her thoughts. "It's never been this personal before."

"Ben would probably have a fit if he thought we were making this much fuss over his death." She smiled to herself, lost in memories. "Then again, he'd probably do the exact same thing if it were one of us."

"He knew you were CIA?"

She laughed, though it wasn't too funny considering how angry he'd been. "About threw a fit over the whole thing. Told me he was Delta Force. What was I supposed to do, but reciprocate? How was I to know he'd hit the roof? Just because he has a team to back him up and I don't."

Sabine pushed away the ache in her chest. She needed

this meeting with her handler, Neil. She had to focus on something that would demand every skill she had, something that would push her to draw deep from her strengths in order to succeed.

She looked at Doug. His eyes were hard, like he didn't want to admit how he felt.

"You agree with Ben?"

He took a deep breath and blew it out. "Can't say the thought of you running around on your own with no support doesn't scare me, because I'd be lying. No...let me finish. I know you're trained. So am I. And they're different businesses, but you can't deny there's an element of danger in our jobs. Both high risk, both requiring intense skill. Can you honestly tell me that you never worried about Ben?"

"No. Of course I worried about him." Sabine tensed. "And with good reason, since he died."

She slammed the door behind her and marched between cars until Doug grabbed her hand and turned her to him. He didn't need to apologize. The look in his eyes took her breath away.

His hand went to her cheek, and then he touched his forehead to hers. "I worry about you. You worry about me. Where do we go from here?"

Sabine leaned her head back. "I'm still going to do my job."

"And so will I."

"To the best of my ability. Yes, there's risk, but I don't put myself in danger more than is necessary. I'm not some kind of maverick just because I don't have a team with me. I follow procedure. I trust the people I work with—" Her voice broke. "I trusted Neil." She shuddered and drew in a breath. "What if Steve Adams was telling the truth? What if I betrayed my country?"

"Did you kill your team?"

"No."

"Did it ever cross your mind that Neil might be lying?"

"That's not a good thing." She stepped away. "If I never considered I was being duped, what kind of agent does that make me?"

"Human?"

"That's unacceptable."

"Seriously? You give me grief for feeling guilty about not doing more when the hard drive exploded, and you think it makes you less of a person to believe that someone's telling the truth?"

"I should have known."

"Sabine—"

"If it's true, this man has destroyed my life. And who do I work for, if not the CIA? The Russians? A terrorist organization? The CIA is going to put me in jail for the rest of my life, Doug. I'm done. It's over."

He grabbed her elbow only enough to get her attention. "This isn't the end. Get it out now, and then go in there and meet with Neil. Look him in the eye and give the performance of your life. Yes, we need to know who you've been passing information to. We also need to know what they know about Parelli's death. But you're not done. You still have some fight left, and I don't believe God would bring you into my life and give me the best shot I've had so far at finding out why Ben was killed and then rip it all away. I can't believe that."

"I need that, Doug. I need one of us to believe, to be completely sure."

"It's not too late. It's never too late."

Not for the first time, Doug wished he could simply will someone else to believe. Just as Ben had been resistant to the truth, Sabine didn't see God the way Doug did. He understood it. Little in their lives pointed to the fact that God was on their side. Witnessing their mom kill their dad and then try to kill them was beyond heavy. Doug wasn't surprised it was difficult for her to trust anyone.

He tucked his hands in his jacket pockets and watched her walk into the entrance closest to the food court.

Ben had done it.

Doug had no doubts that Sabine could come to believe, just like her brother. Ben had seen Doug's life and the way he lived out the things he stood for, even though he wasn't perfect. When Doug had laid out what Jesus had done, dying on the cross, Ben had been blown away. It had been a short jump from there to giving his life to the Lord.

At least his friend had become a Christian in time. It hadn't been too late. Doug could only pray Sabine wouldn't leave it too late, either.

"Excuse me."

Her voice came through his earpiece as she stepped aside for a young mom pushing a stroller. He pulled out his phone and sent Sabine a text.

Got you loud and clear.

Doug checked his watch. He waited for the five-minute mark and then made his own way inside. After buying a corn dog, he chose a spot across the busy food court where he settled at a table with a side view of Sabine drinking a soda.

Two minutes before the cutoff time when Sabine would have stood up and walked away, a man approached. The khaki pants, golf shirt and loafers made him look relaxed, like a retired old man out for eighteen holes of conversation with a buddy. The tweed cap shadowed his face, but

Sabine clearly recognized him since she offered him the seat across from her.

His bearing was familiar.

Doug couldn't place where he knew this guy from and didn't know why he'd expected a younger man. He'd been geared up to instantly dislike the smooth talker who had convinced Sabine that he was a CIA handler. This man was more grandpa than sophisticated deceiver. It was clever, really. Since most people were inclined to trust a harmless old man.

If only Doug could see the guy's face.

"I read your report. I'm concerned about this woman you think was pretending to be you."

Sabine put her elbows on the table and leaned close as he talked in a low voice. "Do you have any idea who she was?"

Neil shook his head. Doug was having trouble reading the man's body language. If he was lying, he was incredibly skilled at it.

"Security cameras from the hotel are grainy, so we haven't been able to figure out who she was. Unfortunately that makes it more likely that the authorities will suspect you, I'm afraid."

Sabine scratched her hairline. "So I was right. They're pinning it on me."

"So what if they do? You're a ghost. If you need to lie low for a while, then stay out of the Dominican Republic. That's not too hard to do. There's plenty of work elsewhere in the world, so we just leave this Parelli thing alone and focus on something different."

"You want me to let this go?"

Doug tensed. Any effort on this Neil's part to push Sabine away from searching for her brother's killer had to be viewed as suspicious.

"I know you want to trace the money from Parelli to whoever originally paid for the hit on your brother, but the hard drive was destroyed. I'm not saying do nothing while the person who killed your brother goes free. I want you to let me work on it. There's a team back at Langley whose only job is to trace that money. As soon as we know something, I'll pass it on. But it's not always possible to get a win, Sabine. You know that. Sometimes you have to cut your losses and move on."

The corn dog didn't settle well. What a pack of lies this guy was spewing. How could they find the person who was behind Neil? When Doug's team got back, he'd have to task the new computer guy to do some checking into the handler.

The kid had navigated them through the hotel to escape those two Italian bodyguards and the police, and he could also unearth information on anyone. California was an exceptional hacker. They needed to trace Neil's phone, get into his email, that kind of thing. Neil was entirely too much of an unknown component for Doug's liking.

"I have a new assignment for you."

Sabine sighed. Doug could see the fatigue wasn't faked. She was genuinely tired. His phone vibrated in his pocket.

"I need some time off, Neil. I've got to get my head straight. I shouldn't have gone on that mission so soon after Ben's death."

Neil patted her hand. "Ben wouldn't want you to push yourself, but neither of us is willing to let his killer just walk."

Doug hated that this guy even thought he was good enough to say Ben's name when Neil had being lying to Sabine for years. Doug could see just how hard this was for her, in the set of her shoulders and the way her fingers were laced.

The woman was trained to project what she wasn't feeling and make it look authentic. If she was giving off tells like that without knowing it, she needed some serious rest.

She sucked in a breath. "What does it matter? Parelli is dead. The hard drive blew up. We might never get to the bottom of what happened. The army isn't going to just hand over the information."

Except that she would likely know before Neil if the army did find out, since Doug would share with her. They needed to know the extent to which Neil was keeping tabs on her. Did Neil know that she'd been with Doug, or even that she had stayed at the general's house?

Neil cocked his head, like he was so innocent. "The soldier you've been spending time with, your brother's teammate. Richardson, isn't it? He hasn't told you anything?"

Neil knew every move she made.

"I think he just feels sorry for me."

Neil nodded. "Stands to reason. If he feels responsible, he might want to help because he feels guilty about what happened. Have you considered that?"

Doug held still. His phone vibrated again, but he didn't pull it out. He caught the eye of an older woman at the next table and nodded politely when inside he wanted to rage that this man had the audacity to question Doug's motives.

"We can get to the bottom of this." Neil put his hand over Sabine's once more. "There are other leads. When you're ready, I'll put you back to work and we'll finish this. It's what you're good at, Sabine."

Tread carefully.

That was what the note had said—the one Sabine had shown Doug on the plane. It seemed that was becoming a familiar refrain.

Sabine held still while the old man kissed her on the head, and then she said goodbye to her mentor. She was valuable enough they didn't want to lose her as an asset, which unfortunately was too bad, since she'd most likely end up in jail for the murder of her team and of Christophe Parelli.

She wasn't sure she'd object to that if it came down to it. After all, she was the one stupid enough to have been duped all these years. She figured she deserved it. Her handler had been convincing, but something should have told her that Neil was deceiving her.

It was so obvious now.

As soon as he had gone down the escalator, she made her way through the mall and bought a coffee, trying to get the bitter taste out of her mouth. She sipped and stared in a store window at a particularly nice blue dress. A shadow darkened the window beside her.

"He's keeping tabs on you."

"Knows every move I make. Probably knew you were here today." She looked over. Doug's eyes were soft. "What do you think?"

"Ditch your phone. Get another that's untraceable. We need to find out everything we can about Neil and who he talks to."

"I'll go over Ben's computer. I haven't had the chance yet, but there could be something on there that might lead us to why someone would go through his room. There has to be a connection."

He nodded. "Agreed."

Sabine turned and leaned back against the store window and took another sip of her coffee. "Did you check on your dad?"

Doug turned and did the same so they were shoulder to shoulder. "On the way over here from the food court. He's awake. The tests were uneventful. He should be released tomorrow, provided he takes it easy and follows up with a cardiologist."

She didn't have the energy to comment, so she smiled. Doug nudged her shoulder with his. "What now?"

"Please, no more airplanes."

He laughed. "Let's go see a movie."

"That sounds amazing."

"Then dinner. After that we'll find somewhere to rest. When you don't look like you're about to fall asleep on your feet, we'll figure out our next move."

And maybe after that, Sabine would have the necessary brain power to figure out why, after years of not bothering, Neil had chosen today of all days to start disguising his appearance.

Later that evening Doug drove back toward the airport. There were decent hotels there, and when they checked in he asked for rooms across the hall from one another. He set Sabine's suitcase down at the end of the bed in her room and watched her take her coat off.

"You look like you might fall asleep if you try to take a bath."

She brushed the hair back from her face. "I'll probably just crash. Thank you for this afternoon. I really needed that break from everything."

"You're welcome."

"Not to mention I might not have the opportunity to go on many dates after I get incarcerated."

"Sabine—"

She shook her head. "It's okay, Doug."

"Seriously? You think it's okay you've lost the will to fight for your life?"

She blew out a breath. "I can't help it if it's inevitable. I'm not giving up. I'm just saying the likelihood of me being free to live my life after the CIA picks apart the last six years is seriously depressing. I told you that I need you to believe for me."

"That won't sustain you. It'll drag us both down. There has to be hope."

"It's slim."

"Slim is okay. It means there's still a chance. And from where I'm standing, there's more than a small chance."

"Truly?"

He rested his hands on her shoulders. "Look, I know you're exhausted, and it's been a good day, so let's not end it on a bad note. I'm just saying impossible things happen all the time. Did you think Ben would ever become a Christian?"

"Never."

"And yet he did."

She nodded. "Okay."

"Text me if you need anything?"

She nodded again.

"Can I kiss you good-night?"

Sabine tilted her face. Doug touched his hands to her cheeks and placed a kiss on her forehead. Her eyes drifted closed.

"Good night, Sabine."

TWELVE

Despite how tired she was, Sabine woke early. After a shower and a cup of bad hotel-room coffee, she decided to look at Ben's computer. When she found the file, she shot up to rush across the hall but saw the clock. She should probably wait until six before she sent him a text.

Within seconds, she got a reply.

Hallway. Breakfast.

They rode in silence to the basement level where the restaurant was. It was quiet since it was so early, which was good because what she had to tell him was important. The laptop loaded while Doug poured and doctored two cups of coffee.

He sat, a frown creasing his forehead. "Isn't that…?"

Sabine nodded. "I got Ben's laptop from the storage unit when we left Seattle."

"Did you get any sleep?"

She shrugged. "I got to thinking about the guy in my house and what he might have been looking for."

"Good thing this was in the storage unit."

"That was Ben. He didn't like being vulnerable." Sabine sighed. She hadn't meant to blurt that out.

Thankfully Doug chose not to pick up on it, instead motioning to the computer. "I'm assuming you found something."

Sabine tugged the small netbook around so they could both see the screen. "He has files of newspaper articles and police reports from the night—" Her voice gave out.

"The night your mom killed your dad."

Sabine nodded. "It's like he was looking for her before he died…for months. He has pictures that look like surveillance photos."

She clicked on a picture of a woman older than Sabine remembered, but still much the same. Dark hair, thick and completely straight, cut to her chin so it framed her face. Sunglasses were pushed to the top of her head, and she had one foot in the back of a limousine like she was getting in or out.

"She looks like you."

Sabine's whole body froze. "What?"

"Or you look like her, however that works."

"I'm nothing like her." She pointed to the screen. "That woman killed the only father I've ever known. For all we know she's responsible for Ben's death, too."

"I'm sorry. I should have thought before I spoke. If there's any resemblance, it's purely genetic." Doug rubbed his eyes. "Is there something here that makes you think your mom killed Ben?"

Sabine's energy deflated. "Strictly speaking, no, but I can't ignore the past. She did try once already. Then there's the fact that he was investigating her when he was killed, digging up buried history. I guess now that I've thought about it, the idea that she's involved in all this won't leave me alone."

"Then we should check it out. Is there anything that will lead us to her?"

"Just the places she's been. Ben didn't know what name she'd been using all these years, so it would be hard to track her electronically." Sabine leaned back in her chair.

"I can't believe he never told me that he was looking for her. I can't even ask him what he was thinking. Maybe he didn't remember what happened the same way I did. He was four years younger."

"It's possible he was trying to find her out of curiosity. Maybe he wanted to get some closure. He never said anything to me about her or what had happened back then. He kept a lot of things close to his body armor."

Doug scrolled through files while Sabine sipped her coffee. Her stomach rumbled, and he squeezed her hand, though his eyes didn't stray from the screen. "Get some breakfast."

Sabine walked to the buffet, picked out cereal and yogurt, mixing the two together with a spoonful of strawberries while Doug studied the photos and muttered.

She sat next to him. "What is it?"

"That's Spain, three years ago. Two days before Sheikh Amad Fashti was murdered in his hotel room. Two Delta Force operators were killed that day." Another picture flicked onto the screen. "This is January of the following year."

"Where is that?"

"Prague. The week before a hotel was bombed, killing more than a hundred people."

Sabine frowned. "That means something to you."

"It shouldn't fit. Maybe it's nothing." He scrolled through more photos. "I wonder if Ben realized."

"Realized what?"

"The Raven was behind all of these incidents. And your mom was apparently right there."

Sabine was about to eat another bite, but paused. "That terrorist you're trying to find?"

"More like international criminal. We're not sure where the Raven's allegiances are. It's easy to call bad guys *ter-*

rorists, but it's not always accurate. Life isn't usually that cut-and-dried."

"What does the Raven have to do with my mom?"

"Maybe it's nothing."

Sabine leaned forward. "Or…"

"Maybe your mom is the Raven."

His words were like being slapped. Sabine jumped out of her seat, ready to defend her mom's honor, and then remembered what she'd seen her mom do all those years ago. She closed her eyes and squeezed the bridge of her nose. There must be something in every person that made them think the best of the people they came from, regardless of whether it made sense or not.

Doug laid his hands gently on her shoulders. She opened her eyes and said, "For her sake, I hope she isn't."

He pulled out his phone. "We'll figure this out."

Doug walked a few paces away. "Yes, sir, I do." He paused a second and then barked out a laugh. "Thanks for the vote of confidence."

He listened for a while and then nodded. "Understood."

When he came back over, he was smiling, like a thousand pounds of weight had been lifted from his chest. "They're already here."

"Who?"

Four guys came in. They were all different body types and had different styles, a fact that had caught her eye before. This wasn't a team cut from the same mold. Each of them was an individual with different skills. The team all scanned the room as they entered. Ben had done the same thing. It didn't matter if they were at a restaurant or walking a street after dark. Safety in the face of constant threat was paramount.

Three of the men she'd met before—Barker, the big Texan; Hanning, the lady's man; and Franklin, whose mom had the best potato salad recipe ever. The fourth was new to her, which meant he was likely "California," the man Doug had spoken to during their escape from the hotel in the Dominican. All of them had bruises on their faces and hands.

They'd been in a fight.

Doug felt like he'd been punched. His team had gone without him, and they came back looking like this? Not that he'd have been able to change the outcome of the mission. It didn't matter that he would have come back looking the same way; it just mattered that he hadn't been with them.

He swallowed the feeling and crossed the room to meet them with a lot of handshaking and some gentle back-slapping.

The new kid, Perkins, who they all called "California" because he dressed like a surfer, looked like he'd been knocked around in a school-yard fight. Barker's breathing was shallow, probably because the Texan had tight bindings on his broken rib. For once Hanning didn't look like he was ready for a photo shoot for a male clothing magazine, and Franklin's inconspicuous-banker look was disturbed by the white bandage over his broken nose.

His team was back. That could be said at least. They were in one piece, which meant the night could have gone a whole lot worse.

"Sit down, all of you. Before you fall down."

No one sat.

Beside him, Sabine shook her head. "You boys look like you need a nap."

"No way." Hanning's chin lifted. "The team is ready and raring to go."

Doug snorted. "Good for you, but you're in luck. It's downtime for the lot of you."

"Downtime?"

Doug nodded. "As of right now, all of us—me included—are officially off the search for the Raven."

Barker moved and Doug braced for it. "I don't believe—"

"Sergeant Barker." Doug moved until his face was an inch from his teammate. "You will sit down before you fall down and you will hold all questions and comments until I have finished what I am saying. Do you understand me?"

"Yes, Sergeant Major."

"Good." Doug gestured to the table and they all sat. Sabine moved away and pulled out enough cups for the men. His heart swelled that she thought to take care of them. "As far as the Raven is concerned, the attempt to dispose of the team was so much of a success and you were all injured so badly that we've been forced to call off missions for the time being. It's vacation for the lot of us. In the meantime, we're switching to alternate identities and we're going to finish this."

"You want the Raven to think we're out of commission."

Doug looked at Barker, who took a steaming mug from Sabine. "I'll give you a moment to catch up, since you have a concussion, but yes."

"Why? We're just now getting close. We're actually onto something if the Raven has resorted to trying to get rid of us. So why stop the progress we're making?"

"Because if the Raven thinks he's bested us to the point that we're giving up, that makes for him to feel added confidence. And confidence makes you cocky. We leak it that we're all recovering from injuries, and once that happens it's only a matter of time before he makes a mistake. One that we will monopolize to the fullest extent of our capabilities. The decision has already been made.

"In the meantime, the CIA knows Sabine has resurfaced. They can't wait to get their hands on her. We all want to find out what the Raven has to do with Ben's death. With what Sabine has found on Ben's computer, we're now closer than ever. Our job is to keep Sabine safe until we can unravel what's going on. Then we can finally get the Raven."

Sabine felt the tap on her shoulder and turned from putting her cereal away. It had taken everything she had not to shout at Doug for making it sound like she couldn't take care of herself. Then she saw he was trying to hold the team together with the sheer force of their respect for him.

Still, she couldn't help saying, "You do know I'm standing right here."

The four of them grinned at her and she smiled back. "Are we done with business now? Can I say 'hello'?"

Despite the fact that Doug had limited his interactions with her to small talk when they had met at team barbecues, the team's acceptance of her had been swift and complete. They didn't hesitate to joke around and make her feel like part of their makeshift family.

Barker swept her up in a bone-crushing hug that lifted her feet off the floor. The Texan's arms were like hams.

Sabine grimaced. "Can't breathe."

He set her down. "Sorry. It's been a long night, but it's good to see you."

"All right, all right, give the woman some room," Hanning cut in. He kissed her hand. "Mademoiselle."

"Aaron." She nodded, mostly to appease him so he would let go of her hand. Hanning always wore designer clothes and could have doubled for a movie star with his blond hair and blue eyes.

Doug was suddenly there, his shoulder in front of hers. "Let go, Hanning. Give her some space."

Franklin adjusted his glasses, the middle-aged banker look firmly in place, despite the broken nose. "So good to see you, my dear."

"You, too. How's your mom?"

He shrugged. "The same."

The fourth man hung back.

Doug waved him over. "This is Perkins. He's—"

She nodded. "Ben's replacement."

"We don't make replacements. California's our newest team member."

The name fit. He really did look like a California surfer. "But he fills what was Ben's role, right?"

"Technically, yes," Doug answered. "He's a good kid."

Perkins shot his team leader a look. "Not a kid."

The kid really was adorable. She had to remind herself he was likely at least thirty, so not more than five years younger than she was. She shook his hand and then turned to Doug. "So what's the plan?"

"The guys eat while we fill them in on what you found on Ben's computer and figure out where to go from here."

Sabine waited until the whole team heaped plates with food and sat back down. "How'd you guys get here so fast, anyway?"

Barker grinned around a mouthful of pancakes. "Our commanding officer made the recommendation that we join you."

Hanning smiled. "Not to mention that following Doug would probably be more interesting than going on vacation, anyway."

Perkins pouted. "I still think we should have gone surfing."

"No, you don't." Hanning cuffed him over the back of the head.

Sabine shook her head over their antics. How did they manage to get anything done? Doug caught them up on the contents of Ben's computer. Hearing the evidence again, she didn't know what she'd do if the Raven turned out to be her mother. Or maybe her mother was just an unwilling pawn in all this. And what about the woman she'd seen kill Christophe Parelli? Sickness roiled in her stomach. She could have been watching her own mother kill someone—again.

If her mother really was an international criminal who discovered that Ben was tracking her, she might have thought he was about to expose her. Perhaps Ben was killed because he had revealed himself, and it meant their mom was finally able to finish what she had started all those years ago, the night she had killed their dad. If that was true, Sabine was left with a truckload of incentive to find her mom and get justice for her brother.

Whether her mom was the Raven or not.

The idea that Ben kept secrets tainted her memory of him in a way she hated. The need to settle this was like a rock in her stomach that wouldn't go away. Surely justice for her brother would get rid of it. And yet there was something in all this that made Sabine think she might never find peace.

Her life was far too mixed up to ever be all the way straight again. She would continually be looking over her shoulder, watching for that moment when everything crashed down again. She would always and forever hesitate before trusting her own judgment.

Doug pushed his chair back and stood. "Let's hit the road."

Sabine grabbed the laptop. "We're leaving?"

"The team is going after the Raven. I have a place you can be safe in the meantime."

"You're going to stick me with your dad while you take down Ben's killer? Doug—"

He came close, his eyes dark and hard. "You're not coming with us."

THIRTEEN

When Sabine pulled out her cell phone before the plane to Washington, D.C., took off, there was a new message.

I have an assignment for you.

She powered down her cell with heavy fingers. "He knows I don't want to work right now."

Doug had his Bible open and balanced on his knee. The volume was no bigger than a CD case, dog-eared and bent like it lived permanently in his back pocket. When he had pulled it out, she'd seen strips of tape across the spine.

He looked up. "What's that?"

She sighed. "You were there. You heard me tell Neil that I wasn't working right now. I can't even consider him or the CIA or my future. I have to put my worry aside until we find the Raven."

"I thought you were going to contact that CIA guy, Steve-something, after you met with Neil. When we met with him you were all about doing surveillance on Neil and finding out who he was, passing it on."

"I know. I just…" Sabine barely had it together enough to focus on justice for her brother. Now that her mom was involved, Sabine was stuck in some kind of self-defense mode, like she was back behind that Dumpster, crouched beside her brother. Trying to convince him everything would be okay, when she knew full well it never would be.

"You gave your word to him, Sabine."

Her heart sank. She had also promised Ben that she would always look after him.

Doug squeezed her arm. "Steve gave us seven days until the CIA launches a manhunt for you. I know it's only been three days, but I won't let us go back on that promise."

At that moment she felt further from Doug than ever before. He didn't understand her at all. He thought she was strong, when in truth she was barely hanging on to the morsel of determination she had left.

Ever since he had dropped the bomb about her not going with his team, there had been a wall between them. She was determined to change his mind. The discussion at the departure lounge of the airport had been awkward to say the least. Every member of his team had seen the tension between them, but no one spoke of it.

Once they were on the plane—which, if you counted all the layovers and detours, totaled nine flights this week—he'd pulled out his Bible. Another reminder of how different they were. Differences that felt somehow insurmountable, since faith was a whole side of him Sabine didn't begin to understand. Nor did she particularly want to know. Not about a God who pointed his finger down from lofty heights and smote people for messing up. The last thing she needed was for someone else to tell her that she wasn't good enough.

She glanced up. There was a question in his eyes. "What?"

"Nothing."

Sabine turned and stared at the carpet of clouds outside her window. They were at cruising altitude now, where the whole world looked like an ant farm. How could God know each and every one of those tiny beings, let alone care about them all?

"He does care about you."

She'd said that out loud? Sabine shut her eyes. How convenient. Doug might not love her, but God did.

Doug looked away so the team didn't think he was crazy, staring at the back of Sabine's head while she looked out the window. He studied the page again. The words blurred.

God, she's so broken, I don't know how to help. Sabine needs You in her life so badly. Show her Your love.

It had been weeks since Doug had prayed with any regularity. Somehow he'd lost the rhythm of daily Bible study and prayer, and it left him off his game more than he had realized. Since the day she had walked into the restaurant where his target was, Doug had been reacting first and going to God second—if at all.

I'm sorry, Lord. I've been trying to figure all this out on my own. If You don't help, this will all go sideways fast. Sabine could get hurt.

The idea of her injured was unthinkable. He was falling for her. He could admit that to himself now, though he hadn't wanted to. And he hadn't needed his dad to say it. Why else would it feel so right to have her beside him? If she wasn't the woman for him, why did he keep having that dream where she was his wife?

God, I want that. I want her in my life. Marriage, kids, the whole package. Only You can figure all this out. I'm trusting You to do that, because she's way too important to me to leave to chance. Help us get the Raven, without Sabine being destroyed in the process.

Doug couldn't begin to imagine a nightmare from his past coming back like that. The horror she'd seen as a child was still with her now. He could see it in her eyes. After years of looking out for her younger brother, Sabine might have lost him to their mother after all. It was a wonder she had managed to hold herself together so well, especially when she didn't know the peace of being able to trust God.

Beside him Sabine shifted in the narrow airplane seat and stretched her neck left and right. It was now or never. She had a right to know what had happened to her brother. To be given the chance to put her fears to rest, even if he would never be able to.

"Sabine?" He cleared his throat. "Honey?"

She turned, and he saw the loneliness in her eyes. Part of him hated that he was about to destroy all the trust she had in him. Once this was done, she would know why they could never be together. Despite how he felt, it was doomed.

It was going to take everything he had for this all to come out the way he dreamed it might, and he didn't have everything to lose. Once she knew he was responsible for Ben's death, it would kill everything she felt for him. She would walk away, and he'd let her, because he wasn't going to be responsible for the death of someone else he cared for. Mistakes cost too much, and he couldn't risk her being another one.

This thing between them couldn't get any deeper; he had to cut if off now.

"There's something I have to tell you."

Sabine listened as Doug told her of a dusty scorcher of a day in some Middle East desert country only weeks ago.

"I was supposed to be the one on point, but something didn't feel right. Ben took charge like I was incapacitated and led the team right into the line of fire."

The anguish in his voice was like a knife to her heart. To see this strong, capable man, whom she cared for, so broken.

"I shouldn't have let him do that. The mission was my responsibility. It was my operation, and it should have been me who went first. One second we're half a klick from the helo, coming up on the end fast, looking forward to going home. The next second we're all diving for cover. Ben was hit in the neck. It was over in seconds."

He sucked in a shaky breath. "It should have been me."

She reached out and gripped his arm. "You can't think that. Ben knew what he was doing. If he disobeyed you and went against protocol, that's on him. It's so hard for me to say that. My baby brother should have been looked after, but that's just the sister in me talking. He was a Special Forces soldier. The best of the best. He was trained, just like you were. He knew the risks."

"But it was my fault."

"Did you fire the gun that killed him?"

Doug looked up from staring at his clenched fists, tears in his eyes. Sabine's chest ached.

"Did you pay the shooter to be there that day?" She laid her hand on his big shoulder and squeezed. "Let's go get the person responsible for it."

"What if it's your mother?"

Sabine shrugged. "She stopped being my mother the day she pointed a gun in my face. There's nothing between us anymore, and I don't want there to be. If she did kill Ben, she's going to answer for it."

Doug took a deep breath and nodded. "I promise you, she will. I'm going to make sure of it."

"So will I. When we face her together."

He shook his head. "I'm sorry. Like you said, we're trained soldiers."

"And my training and ability is tainted because I've been deceived for the last six years?"

"I didn't say that."

"You didn't have to. I can see it all over your face, Doug. You think I'm not up to par because I was tricked. Well, I can match you step for step any day."

"That might be so, but you can prove it another time. You're not coming with us. I have to know you're safe, Sabine. I promised Ben I'd take care of you, and there's no way I'm going to let him down again. I couldn't live with myself."

"So you're tying my hands because of your guilt."

Doug's mouth thinned. "And you're disregarding the way I feel because you don't agree. A bunch of nice words don't erase the fact that Ben's death is on me. There's no way I'm going to let you get hurt, too."

"What about Barker, Hanning, Franklin and Perkins? Aren't they important, too?"

"Of course they are—"

"Then by your own logic, they should stay behind with me. Why don't you just go and bring the Raven in all by yourself, if you're so worried about letting everyone down? Go be a one-man army and bring Ben's killer to justice."

"You know that's not how it works."

"So you'll risk them but not me."

"Because I care about you."

Sabine's heart leapt, despite the fact he'd shouted it at her. She laid her hand over his. "That's good. Because I care about you, too. But caring about someone means you put aside your fear and let them do what they're trained to do. You give them wings. You don't tie them down."

He shook his head. "I can't do it. I won't."

Sabine strode down the gangway into the departure lounge of yet another airport. After a while, destinations and layovers all bled together so she had a general sort of recognition regardless of what country she was in, or what time of day or night it was. She gave a cursory glance to the pack of people sitting around waiting to be shipped all over the world like a crate of apples, each one trying not to bruise the one beside it. She wound her way between exasperated parents and bored business types way too concerned with their smartphones and kept walking.

She barely recognized her life. Everything had changed since Ben's death, and it seemed as if that one phone call had been the catalyst for her whole world to turn inside out. She'd gone from solo covert agent to being shadowed 24/7 by a team of Delta Force operators. Granted, they were hanging back unnoticed, but she still couldn't help feeling smothered by an overprotective detail.

Any other day she might have been able to cover the feeling with the strength of her training. Today it bled into her walk and the painful grip she had on the handle of her rolling suitcase, proving exactly how much of a toll the past weeks had taken.

What was Doug's problem anyway? He thought she was incapable of being any help to their team. If it was her mom they were after, there was no way Doug could justify Sabine's absence.

She had a right to be there.

A flash of color, high and to the right, caught her attention. The widescreen television was on the channel for CNN, and the older man in the picture was one she knew well. She stumbled, and Doug was immediately at her side.

"What is it?" He looked at the TV and sucked in a breath. "That's Major General Taylor."

The anchorman spoke. "The body of this United States Army officer was discovered this morning, washed ashore on the northwestern coast of the French island of Corsica. His family has provided no explanation as to what Taylor might have been doing on the Mediterranean coast, and the army has declined to comment at this time.

"An investigation into the major general's death is forthcoming, and details will be released then. So far the military seems to be keeping a tight lid on exactly what happened."

Neil.

Sabine pushed back the disbelief. The revelation that her handler was in fact a major general with the army was a complete surprise. Of all the coincidences to happen today, her handler found dead wasn't one she'd prepared for.

Doug blew out a breath. "That's crazy. I spoke to him at my dad's birthday."

"He was at the party?" A shudder moved through her. She'd seen Neil—Major General Taylor—less than thirty-six hours ago, in disguise. He'd been at Doug's father's birthday?

Doug looked over at her, his face wistful. "You probably didn't notice him because Taylor would have blended in and looked like any of the other officers there. He was a great soldier and a good friend. Even said he thought of me like a nephew, probably because we've known each other for so long."

At their meeting in the mall food court, he'd made extra effort to disguise his appearance. Had he known Doug was there and needed to keep his betrayal a secret?

She wrestled away the reaction that would have broadcast her surprise. Doug knew her handler, a man who was a traitor to this country? Sabine would deal with this herself. Neil—Major General Taylor—was dead now, so what did it matter if Doug never found out his trust was misplaced?

Doug frowned. "It's kind of funny, though. He actually warned me away from you. Said you would be trouble, that you'd walk away when you were done and I'd have to pick up the pieces. Guess he thought you were some kind of heartbreaker I had to watch out for."

Neil had warned Doug away from her? Had he also thrown that brick through the kitchen window, triggering Andrew's heart attack?

Sabine raised her chin. "I'm sure he didn't know what he was talking about. After all, I've done nothing but conveniently supply you with fresh leads since this began."

His face softened. "I know that, honey. You've been invaluable."

"Then why won't you let me come with you? I won't get hurt. I can take care of myself."

He sighed. "It's not just about your safety. The team's safety is at stake, too. We've trained and gone on operations together for years. Perkins might be new, but he's one of us. You're an unknown component."

"That's unfair! It's—"

"The truth." Doug laid his hand on her shoulder, but she shook him off. "Sabine, each one of the guys has had the exact training I have had. I know every nuance of how they do what they do. In the middle of an op, I can tell you exactly what action they will take and probably what they're thinking. They'll tell you the same about me. Our training exhausts every contingency, every possible outcome. I'm not trying to shut you out. I'm trying to protect you. You're a live wire, and I love that about you."

She jerked back and he snorted. "Don't give me that look. There are plenty of things about you that could make someone fall in love with you. But you're not one of us. I can't put you in the middle of an operation that could change direction at any second and be able to trust that everyone will get out in one piece. As much as I can control what will happen, I am able to say that about my team."

Sabine looked down, understanding what he was saying but not liking it one bit. It wasn't like she was going to jump in the middle and mess up everything. If they laid out a plan, she would stick to it.

"Sabine." He lifted her chin with his fist. "I need you to be safe."

The shame in his eyes melted her heart. She could see the guilt he felt over her brother's death and his promise to Ben that he'd take care of her. She had no desire to put the team in danger but couldn't help how she felt.

"And if you're talking about my mom?"

"The woman tried to kill you. You want to kill her before she gets the chance to finish what she started all those years ago? You want revenge for Ben?"

"I want justice."

"I'll get it for you."

Sabine sighed. "This isn't right."

"Maybe not, but it's the way it's going to be."

Her stomach churned. "So that's it? Your way or no way at all? I can't live like that, Doug. I need give and take. I need a partner, not a dictator always telling me what to do. I need someone who'll stick beside me through everything. Not someone who's one step ahead pointing the way he thinks I should go. I can find my own way."

Doug's hand moved until his palm warmed the side of her neck. She felt herself being tugged toward him, into the shelter of his embrace, and pulled back. "Don't."

He didn't listen. "I don't know if I can be anything other than who I am."

Her heart sank. "So I have to be the one to change? Because I don't believe the same things you do, I'm not good enough?"

"I never said that."

"Well, it's coming across loud and clear." She pulled away.

"Don't do this, Sabine. I'm just trying to keep you safe."
Disappointment was plain on his face, but she ignored it.

"What chance is there for us? We can't agree on anything, so what's the point?" She swiped away the wetness
on her cheek and walked away.

FOURTEEN

Sabine hoofed it through the airport terminal. While she walked, she pulled out her phone and turned it back on as she weaved in and out of people meandering. It immediately buzzed with a new message from Neil.

Terminal B. Gate 32 at 2:35 p.m.

Neil was dead. Who was sending text messages from his phone? Apparently that person knew exactly where she was. She glanced around to find the walkway that would take her to Terminal B and looked for anyone who might be watching her.

She hadn't told Doug about her connection to the dead major general. She probably should have told him she knew his death was tied to what was happening with them—between them.

Doug was determined to protect her. Even now he followed a few paces behind with a heartbroken look on his face that she refused to think about. There was no way she wasn't going to be part of what was about to happen. If it had been her who had died, Ben would have done everything possible to bring her murderer to justice. And her own mother?

Ben loved her and he was dead because of it. Her mom

tried to kill her. Maxwell cheated on her and declared he
never loved her in the first place. She'd been a convenient
wife for him, present in his life but not enough to be a nui-
sance. Doug had said he was falling for her, but showed it
by taking away the only power she had left. If he thought
she would stay out of it, he didn't understand the first thing
about her. She would have to figure out on her own how
to get in on this mission.

Now she had a meeting to attend and less than ten minutes to make it there. She clasped her flower necklace she
wore—a peace offering from Ben—and tried to draw some
strength from his memory.

Task number one: ditch the protection detail.

Doug folded his arms across his chest and stared at the
door to the ladies' bathroom. He couldn't fault Sabine for
hiding in there. She didn't like the way he had pushed her
out of this op. He didn't, either. But, if the unthinkable
happened to her, he would never forgive himself.

Hanning strolled by and raised his wrist, indicating his
watch. Doug gave him an *I know* nod. There was no time
to hang around. They needed to get moving if they were
going to drop off Sabine and get to the meeting they had
scheduled with Colonel Hiller.

A plan had already begun to formulate in Doug's mind.
Using the photos and the information Ben had gathered,
the team would draw the Raven out. Once they had a location, they'd be able to move in and detain him—or her,
if it really was Sabine's mom.

Major General Taylor's death was connected. If it
wasn't, then the timing was entirely too coincidental for
Doug's liking. In his experience, there were no such things
as coincidences.

Something hovered just outside his consciousness, as if

he were trying to grasp a cloud between his fingers. There was some detail about this whole thing that he was missing—something that connected Sabine's handler with CIA agent Steve Adams and the dead major general.

God, help us find the Raven. Let Taylor's death mean something.

Doug kicked away from the wall and tried to look nonchalant instead of on alert. He strolled to the door of the restroom, his mind flashing back to the Dominican Republic. That time he'd been the one in the bathroom, and Sabine had made an effective getaway.

And she was really good at disguises.

He announced his frustration out loud, turning several heads. The cell phone in his hand rang. "Richardson."

"What is it?" It was Barker.

Doug sighed. "Sabine ditched us."

"Girls take a long time in there, doing whatever they do. What makes you think she split?"

He gripped the phone. "Who knows? But I intend to find out. When I get my hands on her, I'll—"

"You were going to leave her anyway. Weren't you?"

"That's not the point." Doug was done arguing about it. "You and Perkins find security and get a look at the recording. She'll be in a disguise. I want to know when she left and where she went."

A young woman with pink streaks in her blond hair exited the bathroom pulling Sabine's suitcase. "I'm out." He ended the call. He jogged over to the girl and swung around so he could cut her off. "Excuse me, ma'am?"

She jerked to a stop, her eyes wide.

"Where'd you get the suitcase?"

The ring in her lip jutted out. "What're you talkin' about?"

Doug folded his arms. "My friend went into the bathroom pulling that suitcase, and you came out with it. I know it's hers. It has her name tag on it."

A. Surleski.

She sighed like Doug was imposing on her. "Fine, some chick gave it to me. What's it to you, anyway?"

"It's important that I find her."

"I get it." She nodded. "You're the stalker boyfriend."

"What? No, she's in danger. She's freaked out, but if I don't find her, she could get really hurt."

The young woman with the pink hair narrowed her eyes. Doug tried not to let his impatience show. Finally the girl found him worthy. "She paid me a hundred bucks to trade bags, but I ain't givin' you the money."

"Which way did she go?"

"I was in the bathroom. How should I know?" She walked away, shaking her head.

Doug called out. "Hey!" The girl looked back. "What color was your bag?"

"Pink tote."

Doug moved. The nearest exit was off the food court that connected the string of gates that branched off from it. He passed the kids' play center and was almost to the gathering of restaurants when his phone rang.

"Richardson."

"Security tapes came up dry."

"Look for a pink tote bag."

Barker sighed. "The image is black and white."

"Assume she's in disguise."

"I thought you were kidding. Fine, we'll check for totes, and a woman with her build."

"Let me know what you find. I'm heading for the exit. Maybe she's leaving the airport and not planning on getting a ticket on another flight."

"Benny's sister really got to you, didn't she?"

Doug hung up. She'd been in black slacks and a red sweater before, hadn't had much time to change, maybe added a jacket and pulled up her hair. She could be wearing a hat.

A woman with Sabine's build and a wide-brimmed hat strode by on high-heeled black boots. Doug grabbed her arm and succeeded in freaking her out, but didn't find Sabine.

God, help me find her. Keep her safe.

Worry churned the remnants of the sandwich in his stomach. It was hard to believe that God might choose to keep her safe by keeping her away from Doug, but he would accept it. He scanned the crowd again.

His phone rang. "Tell me you found her."

"Dark jacket. Hair tied back with what looks like a bandanna, but it's definitely her. She went west, looked like she was with two guys in suits. Tracked her all the way to the exit. She looked in a hurry, but you might be able to catch her on the curb."

"I'm right there."

Doug ducked out the doors and through the crowd that waited for arriving passengers. Now that he knew she'd left the terminal, he could head out there. If he'd risked it, he might have had to come back through the security line when they found her still inside.

He weaved through families, skidded so as to not collide with an old man and had to wait a second for the automatic doors to let him out. The curb was lined with vehicles being loaded. A cop leaned against his squad car with a paper coffee cup.

The fact that she thought she would be better off alone instead of with him freaked him out big-time. There was no way he'd be able to concentrate on apprehending the Raven if he didn't know she was safe.

A hotel shuttle bus pulled away from the curb where they made pickups. Doug scanned the windows for a woman with a cloth over her hair. Beyond where the bus had been was a black Escalade in the far lane. Two men in suits—Christophe Parelli's bodyguards—had their hands on Sabine.

Doug was halfway across the street when shouts erupted and a car horn screamed by behind him. A truck sped into the edge of his vision, and he sidestepped as fast as he could. It screeched to a halt inches from his hip. The cop yelled for him to stop running.

Sabine was almost in the car, being shoved with a hand on her back. Her head hit the door frame. She cried out and turned, and her eyes flew open.

"Doug!" She swung the pink tote at the two men. One of the men grabbed the bag, threw it aside and punched her in the head.

Sabine slumped into the man's arms. Doug was spurred on, narrowly missing another car. He barreled at full speed while they loaded her into the car. The last man climbed in, and the car pulled away before he got the door closed.

Doug braced, prayed and leapt for the open door. His momentum pushed the guy in, creating a tangle of limbs. The car swerved, and Doug gripped the doorframe to keep from falling out. Something pressed into his side and crackled. Just before everything went dark, a heavy accent spoke.

"Maybe we'll get paid double for two of them."

FIFTEEN

The road twisted and turned as it climbed the mountain. Trees lined the edge of the gravel, at least the side that Sabine could see. Her forehead was pressed against the window. Her head pounded from the slam of that fist, and she was about ready to throw up. The press of a large body smashed her against the door. How many people were in the back of this car anyway?

She kept her eyelashes low and hoped they didn't realize she had regained consciousness. She had no idea how long they'd been driving, or where they were headed.

All she could do was watch as her mind replayed the image of Doug running toward her in high definition. That was followed by violent images of them killing her and dumping her body. She tried to remember him in her kitchen, instead. The way his lips moved into a smile and the light of it shone in his eyes.

How would he find her? Did he even want to? She'd hardly been nice to him. The last words spoken between them had been full of frustration over the life she wanted with him, but could never have.

The car slowed and finally pulled to a stop. The landscape was still all trees and the orange glow of sunset. If they'd been driving all afternoon while she was passed out, they could be hundreds of miles from the airport by now. Way out here there was little hope for escape and no one to call for help.

Deep breaths.

She scoured her memory for a time when she'd been in a worse situation, but the pain in her head was too much. Still she hadn't survived being a covert agent for this long without developing some skills.

Think.

A door slammed. Footsteps on gravel rounded the car to her door. When it opened, she started to slide, but football-size hands hoisted her up and out of the car. She was flipped over him fireman-style and her stomach hit his shoulder with every step. She swallowed hard against the nausea as he carried her across the clearing up the wooden steps of a structure.

She couldn't let him get her in the house.

Sabine locked on to his torso with her legs, levered herself up and dove sideways to pull him off balance. They slammed down on the hard wood of the porch. His weight knocked the breath from her lungs. She flipped over as soon as she could move and found herself face-to-face with a .357 Magnum, silver with a black grip.

She swallowed. "Nice gun."

Beyond the barrel of the pistol, the big Italian smirked. "'Tis my favorite."

Sabine stretched out her muscles as she clambered to her feet. Her head still thumped, but a brisk five-mile run through wooded terrain would take care of that. Sadly she didn't get her wish just then, because he poked her in the back with his weapon. She stepped ahead into a small hunting cabin, and the two men crowded in behind her. She turned to glare at them…and froze.

The other Italian hefted a body from his shoulder,

flipped it over and dumped the unconscious man on the floor.

"Doug."

She tried to run to him but thick arms banded around her like a vise. Sabine kicked and squirmed. "I'll kill you. If you hurt him, I'll kill you."

A woman walked up the cabin steps. The urge to fight dissipated from Sabine, and her knees gave out.

The woman's snug black dress outlined a figure that was the blueprint for Sabine's own body. Chocolate-colored hair fell past her shoulders, and her eyes were dark and hard, heavy with smoky eye makeup.

There was no trace of the mother Sabine had known. All that was left now was a woman who had killed her own son.

"Hello, darling. Long time no see."

The Italian bodyguard set Sabine down. She stumbled but forced her shoes to stay planted on the bare wood. She couldn't look at Doug. She couldn't react at all, so she kept any sign of emotion from her face, determined not to let weakness show. The daughter couldn't do anything but react emotionally to what was happening. The covert agent could fight…and win.

"Nothing to say?"

Sabine shrugged, as if reuniting with the long-lost mother who had once tried to kill her was no big deal. She reached up and sought solace from the necklace Ben had given her.

Her mother raised an eyebrow at the sight of Doug unconscious on the floor. "What is that?"

The bodyguard by the door replied in Italian. "He decided to join us."

Her mother huffed and replied in English. "Interesting, since I was under the impression he was recently rendered out of commission in a nasty accident. He looks relatively uninjured to me. I'll have to note that tactic for the future."

Sabine cleared her throat. "Can we get on with…whatever this is?"

A perfectly shaped eyebrow rose. "You have somewhere to be?"

Sabine could name a hundred places she'd rather be. Somehow she'd known this day was coming. The day she would finally face her mother again and have to try to survive when neither her stepdad nor her brother had been able to. Now that it had arrived she felt seriously unprepared to handle what was happening. She had to get herself and Doug out of there.

She swallowed, giving herself a moment to tamp down her emotions. "What's it to you? I doubt you suddenly started to care about my life just now."

Her mom sighed. "I had hoped for the chance to explain a few things to you."

"At gunpoint?" Sabine held back the laugh that wanted to spill out. "Wow, that's one warped sense of atonement you have. You want to make amends so you can have a clear conscience when you kill me?"

"Why on earth would I want to kill you? You're my best agent."

Sabine took a step back. She'd known it, but it was still a shock to hear it confirmed.

Her mother's smile emerged, like a feral tiger. "You've been working for me for years now. You're really very good at your job, Elena."

"It's Sabine."

Her mom waved away the correction. "Details. Anyway, your handler, Neil—"

"The dead major general."

"Very good, and yes, he's dead. Pity, really. He had his uses."

Sabine felt sick. "And my team, six years ago when they were all killed?"

Her mother shrugged. "It was necessary—to make your transition easier."

"It was necessary to ruin my career? The CIA thinks I killed them and went rogue. They're looking for me. I've been under the impression I was an American agent all these years, and now I find out I'm a criminal? How dare you."

Her mom sat on the couch and crossed one leg over the other knee. She motioned to the armchair. "Have a seat, darling, before you blow a gasket."

"I don't want to sit down."

First they had her in the car, now the cabin. If she sat down it would be like taking another step on the plank toward the murky water of her death. The bodyguards both took a step closer, each of their guns pointed at her. Sabine wasn't ready to get shot so she sat and folded her arms. "You expect me to be happy that you did what you wanted with my life?"

Arrogance shone in the older woman's eyes. "You love your job, don't you?"

"I'm supposed to be grateful?" Sabine shook her head, unable to comprehend this woman's audacity. "I'll probably end up in jail for the rest of my life because of what you've done. It was you, wasn't it? You killed Christophe Parelli and made it look like I did it."

Her mother's eyes narrowed. "I hardly think you'll end up in jail."

"How can you be so sure about that? I can't just pick up where I left off and start running missions again. Am I supposed to be some kind of covert agent for hire, doing jobs for whoever will pay the most and living my life with cash and no identity? You may think you have power over me, but you don't." Something clicked in her mind. "I won't turn into you."

Her mother jerked as though Sabine had slapped her.

A tempting thought.

The older woman studied Sabine. "Who said anything about your future?"

"So you *are* going to kill me."

"You said it yourself—the CIA is after you. If you're not going to join me, I can't really afford to let you go. There's no way I can leave loose ends like that." Her surgically perfect nose wrinkled. "Bad for business."

It wasn't a surprise that her mom wanted to kill her. She'd tried it once before. Her mother had no conscience whatsoever. The thought skittered over Sabine like a thousand ants. Once she'd dreamed of home and a family, and while Sabine hadn't been born into the life she wanted, it now looked like she wouldn't be able to make that life for herself, either.

"Is that what Major General Robert Taylor was? A loose end?"

"Your Neil's death was an unfortunate accident. The old man had his charms. I'll miss him."

Sabine saw the first glimpse of humanity then, in her mother's eyes. Would her mom really miss Neil? That would mean she actually had a heart. While Neil might have been lying to her, he had also supported her for years. The man had been both a sounding board and a mentor to her.

Sabine leaned toward her mom. "I'm sorry for your loss."

The woman glared at Sabine. "I don't need your sympathy."

"Good, because I was just being polite. That man betrayed his country because of you."

"Pshaw." Her mom waved her hand. "People will do a

lot of things for the right amount of money…and a little added pressure."

Sabine was nearly sick. "Why?" The word was a whisper.

Her mother blinked, and all trace of emotion vanished from her face.

"Why did you kill Ben…and Dad?" Sabine had to know, since she figured she was as good as dead. Her mom had won, and Sabine didn't care what was going to happen to her, so long as Doug got out of there alive. She just wanted to know why the woman—who was supposed to have kept her and Ben safe, and to have loved their father—could have turned on her own family.

"Life rarely gives a satisfactory answer. You should get used to being disappointed." Her mom stood, then strutted on her spike heels to the door.

"I'm well acquainted with disappointment. I had you as a mother."

The older woman actually laughed. The sound cut off when the front door slammed behind her.

Sabine studied the room. It was a typical cabin, one room with one door at the front. Yellowed single-pane windows, high and small, dotted the walls, but not so tiny she wouldn't be able to dive through one if she got enough of a head start. First she had to get past the two goons with guns.

Not getting shot would be the hard part. After that, her mother would be easy pickings given the rage that burned inside Sabine. All the deaths her mom was responsible for—it was so senseless.

Doug lay motionless on the floor. If he was still unconscious, he must be really hurt. She'd already shown them how much she cared for him by exploding when they had dumped him on the floor. This was going to be even more difficult if she had to protect him, fight two big Italian thugs and drag Doug's prone body out of the cabin.

Sabine refused to admit defeat when she was perfectly able-bodied, in full possession of her faculties and had the skill that was borne of her training plus the brain God had given her. She refused to be just another statistic on her mom's vast résumé of crimes.

God, I want to live.

She wasn't even sure how it would help. Not to mention that a sudden conversion when the end loomed near seemed a little too cliché. She always mulled things over—to death, if you'd asked Ben. She wasn't one to make rash decisions on something as important as devoting her life to a religion.

Then again, the track record of her decision making so far wasn't all that great. Her marriage to Maxwell had been an unmitigated disaster, and she'd held him off for months before she had agreed to get engaged. Weeks later they'd been married. He had probably sped up the timetable so she didn't have time to change her mind.

If she prayed to God to get her out of this, she'd have to keep her end of the bargain when He did. Was she ready to change her whole life just on the off chance that Doug was right? Would everything really be better if she gave it to God?

She looked at the two bodyguards. Any idiot could pull a trigger and kill someone. It didn't matter if they had good aim or not, these guys could end her life. How could God make this situation any different? Her mom would either kill her now or make her suffer first. Either way she was still dead. Doug had to get out alive. That was a promise she made to herself.

God, I don't care what I have to do. I believe in You. That's not the problem. Doug says You love me, but I don't understand how You could or why. I don't expect You to get me out of this, but help me save Doug.

Maybe it was even more of a cliché to give her life to a God she didn't know and didn't understand only because she needed help, but she would have done anything just then. Although if she could have a minute when he was conscious to say sorry for walking away and trying to ditch him again, she'd take it.

Doug probably thought she was a horrible person, duping him for a second time. If it had been her, she would have left him after being given the slip twice. She wasn't one for taking chances and trusting people. Hopefully Doug was more forgiving than she was.

Sabine reached up once again and gripped her flower necklace. The petals were warm from her body heat, and she felt a surge of reassurance. She felt Ben's presence in her memories like the phantom pain of a limb that had been amputated.

God, help me.

Footsteps crunched the gravel outside as her mom moved around the exterior of the cabin doing…something. The guard by the door let his attention flick to the window.

Sabine seized the opportunity. She kicked him and grabbed his gun as he fell. The other gun fired as she spun. The bullet sliced through the muscle of her left shoulder, and she gritted her teeth but held on. Two shots from her gun and he dropped to the floor, groaning.

The first guy's arms wrapped around her from behind. "You'll pay for that."

He squeezed the breath from her lungs and lifted her off her feet. The pain in her shoulder brought black spots to the edge of her vision. He should be permanently down, but Sabine didn't have time to figure out how her aim had been off.

There was a rush of movement behind her and the guy went limp. They both fell to the floor. She slammed into him, and her breath whooshed out.

A hand was stretched out in front of her face. Beyond it, Doug smiled. Sabine shoved the guard's arms from around her middle and let Doug haul her to her feet.

There was the unmistakable sound of a gun being cocked. All sign of life bled from Doug's face, and his eyes turned to the eyes of a warrior. Something small and unyielding touched the back of her head, and she froze.

"You move and she dies."

SIXTEEN

"Hello, Raven." Doug stared at the woman who had destroyed Sabine's family, most likely had killed a respected major general and was either a conspirator or accessory to so many other crimes that it would take all day to list them. It wasn't his life that flashed before his eyes in that moment; it was the life he might have had with Sabine. It was the *maybe*.

The older version of Sabine snarled. "Clever boy."

Doug stepped back and put one foot of space between him and the two women. The Raven had been outside. Doug had been so intent on saving Sabine that he'd let his guard down, and now she was going to pay for it.

Sabine's eyes flashed, but Doug simply couldn't stand to lose the promise that he saw when he looked at her. There was no way he was going to let her die. His entire world had been thrown upside down by a beautiful woman. Ben's sister. She had become more to him than he'd ever imagined, a vital part of his life.

"Now—" the Raven's eyes tracked his retreat "—my daughter and I are going to walk out of here. You don't follow us, and I don't catch even a scent of you, or she's dead. Understand me?"

Doug nodded.

Tears streamed down Sabine's face and blood soaked the fabric of her shirt on her upper arm. Doug shook his head, tried to communicate to her that everything was going to be fine. He would find her. He loved her.

Anything other than her safety was unacceptable. And it would destroy him.

God, go with her.

It took everything he had not to run down the cabin steps and tackle the Raven, but he couldn't put Sabine in that kind of risk. He had to wait. He'd thought the Raven intended to kill Sabine. From their conversation, it had sounded like the older woman planned to kill both him and Sabine. So why take her now? It made no sense. Far worse than a cold and calculating enemy was one who acted irrationally and without logic.

Doug stood immobilized while Sabine's mom marched her from the cabin to the SUV parked outside. As part of his heart got farther and farther away, he reached for every ounce of training he'd ever had. He needed his team if he was going to pull off the biggest mission of his life. If he was going to have any hope of getting her back.

The Raven, her gun still at Sabine's temple, pulled out a cell phone. Doug's brain spun, like wheels that suddenly found traction. She'd been outside doing something.

There was a shimmer in the air. Wind rushed through the open door, and he started to run for the back of the cabin. He launched himself through a window, over the rear porch, with a wall of hot air behind him, and hit the grass with a grunt.

Wind whipped Sabine's hair as a roar launched from the space behind her. The cabin exploded into a fireball that launched flames and smoke into the air. Her mother spurred her to the car.

"Maybe you do have your uses. After all, you saved me the trouble of having to plant the evidence you killed those two Italian idiots and your boyfriend. I'd already set the explosive charges when you decided to play hero-spy-escapes-the-evil-abductors. Even if you did ruin the plan that you die in there with them." She shrugged. "Oh, well."

Hands gripped Sabine under the arms. "In we go."

She cried aloud and almost passed out as the pain radiated from the gunshot wound in her shoulder. She stumbled but her mom held her weight, hauled Sabine's limbs onto the front passenger seat and slammed the door.

"No." Sabine's voice was barely a whisper. She tried to grab the door handle, but her fingers wouldn't cooperate. Nothing was working. Where were they going? What was her mom going to do with her?

Her mom slammed the driver's door and started the engine. A feral noise emerged from Sabine's throat. Doug had been in the cabin. He was dead. She squeezed her eyes shut and willed away the rush of tears.

Her mom grabbed her around the shoulders. Her hand pressed directly on the bullet wound on Sabine's upper arm. "Don't worry, darling. We're together now."

Sabine didn't have time to cry out before the world went black.

Hours later Doug sat on a crate in a Baltimore warehouse. He wanted to pace out his frustration, but the team was all giving him the same look—the one that said, *Sit down already. You're making us crazy.*

He exhaled, but it didn't help to dissipate the pain in his limbs. His head still throbbed from when he hit the ground after jumping through the back window of the cabin. He didn't even want to think about the glass cuts on his hands.

Colonel Hiller sat across from Doug, his pressed suit

and combed hair a contrast against the dust and grime of the warehouse. "Perkins's job is to get everything he can from Ben's computer. Everyone else knows what to do. And regardless of what some people think—" he shot Doug a look "—I'm not giving you the runaround. We will find her."

Doug tried to believe that. He had to believe it, because he was scared to death that, if he didn't, there wouldn't be anything left for him.

Father, I need Your help.

He loved her, more than anything. More than his job even. She'd walked away at the airport because of it. Now, after he'd found her, she was gone again. Like sand falling between his fingertips. The missions his team undertook might be important work, but her life meant so much more to him than any of it. Sabine was everything. And it was tearing him apart that he'd realized it too late.

Please don't let it be too late.

Colonel Hiller was still talking. Doug tuned in to what he was saying.

"—can't forget this woman is a trained agent. She can take care of herself. We want to save her for Ben's sake, because she's his sister. It's tempting for us to think we're the only ones who can get her out of this because of who we are. We know what we're capable of, but Sabine is good. I read her CIA file. Even six years ago she showed excellent promise."

Doug had fallen back on his training. He'd tracked her across the airport and still hadn't been able to save her from being taken by those two Italian bodyguards. Guys he'd last seen working for Christophe Parelli; guys who'd died, unconscious, in the cabin fire.

Another puzzle piece in the mystery of the Raven had fallen into place.

The two Italians had become reemployed entirely too fast not to have had close ties with the Raven even before Parelli's death. A good lead, one that could prove useful, but it didn't wash away the sting of Sabine being taken… again.

Mistakes piled on top of mistakes. He hadn't thought he could take any more failure, and here it was again. All that reliance on his training had been useless. Doug's instincts were of no help. Sabine was gone, and the way it sliced at him left him wide open, tasting bitter defeat.

A piece of paper was shoved into his hands. Doug looked up. Hanning's movie-star looks held a distinct shadow. "This wasn't your fault."

Doug saw differently in his friend's eyes. "That doesn't get her back."

"You know what will?" Colonel Hiller stepped into view beside Hanning. "We run this down like any kidnap victim we're going after. Stop moping around, and let's get to work."

Doug looked at the paper in his hand. "Wasting our time with phone records?" He stood up and got in the colonel's face. "And pep talks? Like a motivational speech is going to help. Sabine could be dead already, and you think we're going to find her by sitting here?"

"We know you love her." The colonel's voice was measured, as if he held back what he really wanted to say— probably a reprimand for talking that way to a superior.

Doug sat down. There was a time when he had lived to run down the target and save the life of the innocent person stuck in the middle. But no more. The love he had for his life disappeared around the same time as Sabine. Now he had a new dream, one that featured that very same woman as a key player. He needed to find her so he could tell her. So he could apologize for failing and promise it would never happen again.

He put his face in his hands, vaguely aware of the team and the colonel discussing repeated numbers on Major General Taylor's phone records.

"I got an interesting delivery this morning. From Steve Adams."

Doug lifted his head. "CIA agent Adams?"

The colonel nodded. "Disappeared three days ago. Flew to the south of France and vanished."

"The south of France again. What was in the package?"

"It was one of those 'in the event something has happened to me' deals. Full of records, such as a copy of a passport for Neil Larson with Taylor's picture."

Doug's eyes widened. "Larson?"

"Major General Taylor's wife's maiden name, of all things. Not very original, if you ask me, but there you have it."

"What else?"

The colonel held up a grainy photograph. "Copies of call records for Neil Larson's cell phone, listing some very interesting numbers, including your girl and a Brenda Sanders."

Doug's breath caught. "The Raven. Sabine's mom."

"One and the same."

"I told you all this already! How does this help us find her? The woman killed her husband and Ben. Who's to say she won't just shoot Sabine and disappear?"

Colonel Hiller's mouth pressed into a hard line. "She's had plenty of opportunity. We're banking on the fact that, since Sabine has worked for the Raven all these years, Sabine will either be valuable to the woman or she'll be given enough freedom that she's able to get away to a phone to call for help."

"If she wants to."

Everyone turned, and Perkins found himself suddenly the center of attention. Ben's laptop was perched on his knees.

Barker smacked Perkins on the back of the head. "Why would you say something like that?"

Perkins winced. "The colonel said it. She's worked for the Raven for six years. Maybe all this is a ploy to go and work for her for real, but she's making it look like she's being forced. Do we know for sure she's legit? All the evidence says Sabine killed her whole team six years ago. Maybe she really did go rogue."

Doug surged forward. "How can you say that?"

Hanning and the colonel grabbed Doug's arms.

Perkins shrugged it off. "I'm saying we don't know for sure. She could be one of them now. I don't think we should ignore the possibility."

"We can." Doug clenched his jaw shut. "And we will. There's no way Ben's sister has gone to work for the Raven."

Perkins put the laptop aside and stood. "Your opinion of Ben is clouding your judgment of this woman."

"You think I don't know her? You think I'm not capable of knowing whether someone is being honest or if they're just stringing me along?"

"She's a woman. You're telling me that you've never let—"

Doug was ready to explode. "You'd better stop right there, California."

Perkins was about to shoot something back, but Colonel Hiller got between them. "Perkins, thank you for your incredible distrust of all women everywhere. We will take it under advisement, but your job is that computer and nothing else." Perkins sat back down.

Barker slapped him on the back of the head again. "Hey!"

Barker scoffed. "Get back to work."

"I already found something."

Doug, the colonel and Hanning all surged forward. "Well?" Doug was about to wring it out of him. "What is it?"

Perkins turned the laptop around on the crate so they could see the screen. "Ben had a whole folder labeled *Sabine.*"

"And?"

"You see this?" Perkins pointed to a program icon on screen.

"What is it?" Colonel Hiller looked about ready to lose it.

"A GPS program."

Doug frowned. "Ben had his sister bugged?"

Perkins nodded.

"The flower necklace. It was a gift from him."

"If it's active, then we can find her." Perkins clicked on the program, and they all stood silent while it loaded.

A map of North America popped up on the screen, a satellite image. A red dot hovered over West Virginia. Doug held his breath while the map zoomed in, closer and closer.

The screen went black.

"What just happened?"

Perkins didn't answer. He started tapping buttons in what looked to Doug like a frantic panic to get the map back. Nothing happened. A cursor appeared on the screen. It flashed a couple times and words started appearing, like someone typing on the keyboard.

You'll never find her.

"Perkins—"

"It's not me. Someone hacked this computer or the GPS

program. When we activated the search on Sabine, we tipped them off."

Doug turned to the colonel. "The Raven."

"Seems like it." There was no hope in his senior officer's eyes. "She's gone."

Doug strode from the warehouse to the vehicle he'd rented. He climbed in, slammed the truck door and hung his head until his forehead touched the steering wheel.

His phone rang. "What?"

"Everything okay, son?"

He sighed. "Not really, Dad. I'm kind of busy."

"I wouldn't be asking if it wasn't important. Major General Taylor's body is arriving tonight. You know he was a friend of mine. I'd be there to greet him myself, but, if I leave the hospital, I'll never hear the end of it from Jean."

"You're not well enough to put yourself under that much stress." Doug frowned. "Wait…what do you mean the hospital?"

"I might have…sort of…"

"Dad—"

"Had a little issue earlier. But it's nothing. They're just adjusting my medication."

"Don't go anywhere. I'll meet Taylor's body for you."

Despite everything that was happening, Doug would do this favor for his dad. He didn't want to think about the old man being anything other than the energetic father he'd always been. The general needed rest so he could get back to being his old self.… Doug couldn't let his dad find out Dad's old friend and colleague had been involved with the Raven.

The sun gave way to the black of night before Sabine allowed herself to comprehend what had happened. She flexed her bound hands and drew her knees up to her chest.

The nasty motel headboard wasn't pleasant to lean against, but that was the least of her worries.

Her shoulder throbbed under the tight bandage. Her mother had threatened to sew the wound together herself. But she'd backed away fast when Sabine had screamed loud enough to alert all their motel neighbors. With no anesthetic and a lack of sterilized utensils, Sabine wasn't about to let anyone near her arm, least of all a crazy woman.

"That should hold them off for the time being."

Sabine could admit to a certain curiosity about what her mom was talking about, but wasn't going to let her know that. Instead, Sabine turned her head and stared at the curtain that blocked the view outside.

"Your man's team. Did you know they tried to convince me that they were all incapacitated?" Her laugh was high and piercing. "Now he's gone, and they'll never find you. I've made sure of it."

Sabine should have let her mother sew up her arm. Dying from an infection would probably be more pleasant than having to listen to this.

Sabine looked back at her, not caring that all the despair she was feeling was probably right there on her face. "What do you want from me?"

The gleam in her mother's eyes made her look like an unhinged lunatic. She crossed the room and yanked the necklace from Sabine's neck, tossed it to the ground and stomped on it with the heel of her shoe.

"We're a team, you and I. From now on it's us against the world. We're going to finish what I started. There won't be anywhere in the world where people won't know what you and I have done." She grinned. "It's going to be incredible."

"You were going to kill me."

"Please." Her mother rolled her eyes. "That was never the plan. We're going to make a name for ourselves."

The woman was crazy, flip-flopping back and forth. Did she even know what she was saying? Now instead of dying, Sabine was supposed to be a terrorist? Or some kind of traitor to her country? The idea tore apart what was left of her heart. The CIA already thought she was guilty of multiple murders and betraying her country. After this they would have irrefutable proof. They would never believe she was innocent now.

She forced herself to push back the panic and breathe easy. "What have you done?"

"We haven't done it yet, silly. We're going to do it tonight. The clock's already ticking." Her mother cocked her head, looking at Sabine like she was a small child. "We're going to bomb the CIA, of course. And those military snobs, who think they're so perfect. At the exact same time. That's the beauty of it. I finally figured out that selling weapons was only part of my destiny. I'm going to finish my enemies once and for all so they never find us."

"From a motel room?"

"Why not? No one will expect it. They'll just be all boo hoo, so sad they're dead. Poor Taylor. Poor Agent Adams."

Sabine jerked. "Steve Adams?"

Her mom nodded. "Don't you know? You killed him, too."

Three hours later

Uniformed soldiers flanked the aircraft as the body of Major General Robert Taylor was carried from the plane. The casket was covered with a flag, the white stripes gleaming under the harsh glare of the lit runway. Doug stood beside his teammates as the procession emerged from under cover of the plane's tail.

With a blinding flash and a deafening crack of thunder, the world went black.

SEVENTEEN

"What happened here?"

Doug didn't have to know the guy; his whole manner screamed CIA. After being blown back by the force of yet another explosion, Doug's hands were still shaking. The dissipation of adrenaline left him antsy and itching for a fight. "The casket of Major General Robert Taylor was the source of the explosion."

Dressed in a dark suit and plain red tie with his hair gelled back, the CIA guy's eyes widened. "Fire marshal went through here already?"

Doug took a cleansing breath. "No. I saw it myself." The shock of the explosion had blown them off their feet. Perkins had a concussion from hitting the tarmac, and Doug's head still hadn't stopped pounding. Again. "Most likely they'll find a bomb was planted in the casket. Whether or not the major general's body was also in there remains to be seen."

The CIA agent pulled a cell phone from the inside pocket of his jacket and turned away.

The whole tarmac was a flurry of activity. Firefighters, police and military personnel walked back and forth, trying to make sense of what had happened. The injured had all been taken away in ambulances. This was the last thing Doug expected when he was only here as a favor for his dad. He could hardly believe what he'd seen, and his army life so far had been a long one.

The thought of retirement entered his mind, not entirely unwelcome. Being a team leader had been an exhilarating experience where every minute was different from the last. Years of training had left him with calluses on his hands and his mind from the repetitive action of attack and defend.

And he would give it all up if it meant finding Sabine. If it gave them a shot at the something wonderful he already knew existed between them.

"Confirmed. Did we figure out the source of the other explosion yet?" The agent listened for a minute. "I'm on my way. Tell everyone. No one goes home until we find the Raven. Both of them."

Doug had been about to walk away but turned back. "What was that?"

The guy slid his phone into the inside pocket of his jacket. "Classified CIA business. We don't share, especially not with people who associate with known enemies."

Everyone seemed so intent on thinking Sabine was the bad guy. Someone had to be on her side. "You're gonna share with me."

She was used to being alone. Doug didn't know why he couldn't trust her self-sufficiency. There was too much about her that made him want to protect her. She might not like that she brought out his hero-of-the-hour instincts, but that was the nature of what he felt for her. She wasn't just a kidnap victim.... She was his.

She was strong, fierce and brave. He couldn't help loving her. She held his heart in the palm of her hand, and all Doug wanted was the chance to tell her that.

"We know all about your relationship with Elena Sanders." The CIA agent got in Doug's face. "Given the suspicion she's under, you have to know the position that puts you in. Someone who consorts with the Raven surely has bad judgment. I'd watch yourself, Sergeant Major Richardson, before all the hard work you've put in over the years gets thrown away because of a woman."

"Sabine isn't the Raven. Her mom is."

The agent's eyes gleamed like he'd won a prize. "Not according to an email sent to every news agency in the country an hour ago. The Raven, a mother and daughter team, have claimed responsibility for both attacks."

"Both—"

"If you see or hear from Elena Sanders, this woman you call Sabine, you are to contact the CIA immediately or you will be aiding and abetting a fugitive. It was her work that caused the carnage you see around you, the loss of American lives. Honorable men and women who serve their country. You ought to know something about that. The son of a general, a Special Forces soldier—"

"How do you—"

"We will find Ms. Sanders and bring her in. Dead or alive. Rogue agents cannot be left to run loose. They must be dealt with swiftly and precisely, regardless of your feelings for her. Your obligation to this country means that, if you see her first, it's up to you to take care of the matter."

He strode away, and Doug wished he could let go and pummel something until he collapsed. It wouldn't help. Everything he wanted was being ripped away. Sabine's reputation was trashed. Even if they could prove her innocence, she would never be free to live her life. She would always and forever be under suspicion.

Hanning trotted up beside him. "Now we know why the colonel got that package from Steve Adams."

"Why?"

"His body arrived at Langley the same time that Taylor's got here. Adams's casket blew up the delivery guy, his truck and the security guards the same time the bomb here in the major general's casket went off."

Doug hissed.

"There's more. Colonel Hiller found something. He wants us on a plane to France. Now."

Sabine sat on the bedroom floor aboard the yacht. The carpet was thin, and the plastic wire on her wrists cut into her skin. She had no idea where her mother was. After tying Sabine up, the Raven had piloted the boat out into open water and lowered the anchor. Who knew what she was doing now? Across the room a small TV was tuned to news coverage.

The TV show was broadcast in French so she had to piece the story together from what words she understood, along with pictures of the wreckage and the look on everyone's faces.

Two pictures came on screen—her own and an old shot of her mom from years ago. This was it. She was actually being associated with her mother. And for something she had no knowledge of. It looked like a couple of pretty big explosions. That much carnage surely meant innocent people were dead.

God...

Sabine let the tears come. Tears for Ben and everything he hadn't felt he could share with her, for him looking into their past and trying to move on. If she hadn't known it already, the huge step he'd taken in dealing with the past would have convinced her how strong he was.

More tears came. For everything she should have had. Things she'd lost. Things that had been taken from her. For Doug and the relationship they would never get to have.

For not having had the courage to trust him, to love him sooner. Before it was too late.

Sabine cried for the kind of love Doug would have showered on her. He'd have made her feel accepted for the first time by a man other than her brother.

And she cried for the loss of a life full of love and laughter…marriage and kids.

It didn't matter now that they would have had to fight to stay together and manage to overcome the obstacles life had put between them. All that mattered now was the dream of what could have been.

God…

She didn't know what to pray, or what she could possibly ask God to do that would make this all go away. Everything honest and upright in her wanted to scream at the injustice of it. She had lived so long in the shadows. Now that everything about her was being called into question, there was no one to vouch for her.

Maybe it was the pain in her shoulder, or the wooziness of being drugged and flown halfway across the world until she didn't know if it was day or night. Not to mention she hadn't eaten anything in more than a day. All of it made her brain come up with some pretty crazy thoughts.

Sabine blinked and tried to focus on something else. It was that or go around and around again. It was all over for her. No one would ever trust her now. She couldn't even trust herself after being duped so completely. Her last act should be one of honor if she was ever going to repair her reputation, not to mention the side effect it would have on Ben's reputation. Even though he was dead, she still couldn't stand for people to think badly about him. And Doug—his judgment would be called into question for believing in her.

There it was.

Rid the world of a woman bent on evil and destruction. It was the one good thing Sabine could do. She wasn't going to be able to fight much longer before her mom snapped, frustrated because Sabine wouldn't do what she wanted her to.

Better to kill her first.

She thought she could pull a trigger on the woman who'd destroyed her life. After all, Brenda Sanders had never really been a mother to her. Not to mention the countless others her mom had killed or people whose lives she had destroyed.

The world would be a better place without the Raven in it.

God would forgive her. Wouldn't He? There had to be some justification for murder, some time when it could be right. Otherwise Doug would never have become a soldier. His honesty and high morals would never lead him into a job that was at odds with what he believed.

A rustle at the door brought her head up.

Brenda came in, her body vibrating and glee in her eyes. Sabine wanted to throw up. She had to get her hands on a weapon, but there was little she could do tied up. She would have to make this believable. She swallowed and made her voice quiet. Hollow. "What have you done?"

Her mom blinked. "We, dear. We killed a bunch of military people and CIA types."

Sabine's stomach clenched. She had to convince the woman she was just as crazy. "There's nothing left for me." Tears spilled onto her cheeks and her heart ripped out all over again as she remembered the cabin exploding. "It's all over."

Her mom had to believe she'd joined the cause because it was the only thing left. She had to think Sabine had no intention of retaliating. Sabine lifted her bound hands.

Raw, they sliced with pain at the movement. "Cut me free. I want to die."

Her mom crouched in front of her and touched her hands. "You don't want that, darling."

"Yes, I do. I have nothing to live for. My reputation is in ruins. Everyone I love is gone. Let me die."

"I'll take care of you." She stroked Sabine's fingers. "Everything will be better. You'll see. We can go somewhere sunny, and you can work on your tan."

Sabine wanted to slap her. Instead she held still while her mom produced a knife.

Her mom hesitated. She shifted the knife in her fingers and then pulled back. "I think I'll wait. I don't want you to harm yourself. We'll leave you tied up a little longer."

Sabine sighed aloud. "Whatever you think is best." She could tell her mom was surprised, so she kept her eyes lowered. "Could I get some water?"

"Sure, darling."

Bingo. Her mom went to get her a drink.

And left the knife on the floor.

Doug adjusted the binoculars to focus better on the yacht. Prayer hadn't been far from his lips during the whole plane ride. Or the time it had taken them to flash the Raven's picture around at the harbor and find out which boat was hers.

Now they were a mile offshore, hidden by the dark, cloudy night. Watching.

"Let's move in."

"MacArthur—"

He ignored Perkins. "The debate is over. It's time to execute. I want Sabine out of there and the Raven in custody before the CIA gets anywhere near here."

None of the guys said anything; they just nodded and

gathered up their stuff. The small boat barely held all their gear and weapons. It bobbed around, dangerously low in the water. He prayed they would continue to go unnoticed in the middle of the Mediterranean with their engine silent.

Doug was the first to slip into the water. The swim was swift and silent. Hanning appeared beside him at the yacht where he gave Doug a boost that launched him up and over the side of the boat. He immediately crouched to make sure no one had been alerted to their presence and then pulled the next man up until the five of them were on deck.

Someone screamed.

Five weapons were suddenly more than ready to take care of whatever situation was in front of them. No words, no instruction was needed. Each man simply turned to his task, the procedure already firmly laid out in their minds.

Doug met no resistance, not a soul between him and the closed door to the bedroom. There was a thud, and the scream rang out again. This time he was certain it was Sabine.

Hanning appeared behind him. Doug stepped back, his weapon trained on the door while he reached in his pocket. His teammate kicked the door in. Doug threw a flash-bang. A split second later, he entered the room.

Sabine wrestled with the Raven. Both of them gripped the knife as they fought for ownership of it.

"Down!" Doug yelled.

Sabine reacted instantly to his command. She hit the floor, arms curled over her head. The Raven launched at him from the far side of the bed, her eyes wild, and the knife in one hand. He didn't have to think to aim his weapon. He just flexed his trigger finger and the Raven was no more.

Doug crouched beside Sabine and drew her arms down. She had deep gashes on her wrists and a bruise on the side of her face. Her left shoulder was bound with a thick bandage soaked with red. Eyes, wide and full of tears, looked up at him, and the sight of it broke his heart.

"Sabine."

He got his weapon out of the way before she wrapped her arms around him and burrowed her face in his chest. "Thank You, God. Oh, thank You, God."

Her words were a prayer. Her breath came in great heaving sobs. Doug's heart felt like it grew wings, knowing she had placed her trust in God. Doug would give anything to never have to leave her again. "Sabine, it's me. I'm okay."

"The cabin…"

Doug leaned back and held her face in his hands. Tears streamed down her cheeks and wet his palms. "Honey, I'm so sorry." He swiped away a tear. "I'm so sorry."

She sniffed, brokenness written on her face. "You were dead."

His stomach flipped over. "I'm sorry."

"I realized I loved you."

"We'll take it from here." Suited agents surrounded them the minute they stepped off the plane. Behind them stood other suits with dark blue jackets as well as regular police officers, all with their weapons drawn. Doug had known his time with her would be limited, but he'd vainly hoped for more than this before Sabine was whisked away for questioning.

In a last-ditch effort, Doug had pleaded with her not to get on the plane but to disappear into the world with him. They could live their lives together. She had stubbornly refused to run, telling him in no uncertain terms, "I have to answer for what I've done."

He loved her more in that moment than he already did. Faced with the reality of it now, Doug felt her shake be-

side him. Being careful of her freshly bandaged arm, he
brought her against him. His lips touched her forehead,
the softness of her hair.

I loved you.

He would get her to admit she loved him now, and not
just when she'd thought he was dead.

Tears filled his eyes, but he didn't care. "I'll see you
soon."

She sucked in a breath. It probably would have been a
sob, but for the sea of people surrounding them. She pulled
away and looked up at him. Her eyes were dry.

"Sabine—"

She brushed back a lock of her hair and stepped away.
"Goodbye, Doug."

Doug forced himself to stay put while she walked to
the agents. What if he never saw her again? It was useless to believe she would ever be a free woman. The CIA
would lock her away for her connection to the Raven. For
being unable to prove she hadn't been in league with the
woman all these years.

*God, help us. There has to be hope, and it can only
come from You.*

In Doug's own strength he would just fail. Only God
had the power to bring it all in line so that Doug and Sabine could be together. And he had to believe that they
would. Why else would he keep having that dream—the
one where he walked in their house, and she took him into
her arms? The dream where his ring was on her finger and
her tummy was round with his child?

Please, Lord.

"Murderer!"

Doug rushed to Sabine before it registered in his mind
that the middle-aged man in the trench coat had burst
from the crowd.

Who was he?

A clatter of gunfire erupted from the man's AK-47. Doug had Sabine shielded with his body when the stab of fire hit his chest, and she screamed.

EIGHTEEN

Sabine lifted her head from the cold metal of the table. "I understand how it looks, but what I'm telling you is the truth. My mother—the Raven—who I hadn't seen in over twenty-five years before a couple of days ago, she orchestrated this whole thing."

The room was bare. Plain walls, fluorescent lights and a single window that only reflected back the picture of her and the agent performing the interrogation. She had no idea where she was being held. The agent looked calm and collected, while Sabine sat there, dirty and sweaty, wearing the same clothes she'd been in for two days now. She probably stank to high heaven, but she couldn't smell it anymore.

"Then you understand my dilemma, Ms. Sanders—"

"It's Ms. Laduca. Sabine."

It might be a small thing, to quibble over the name she'd been given by her mother versus the name she had chosen for herself. Ben's last name. She had to hold on to the things she could control. She had to grasp the thing that gave her peace. Especially when she couldn't stop reliving the moment when the man she loved had shoved her out of the way and had taken a bullet for her—in his chest.

His chest.

She still couldn't help thinking about what she'd seen in his eyes as he lay there, bleeding out on the carpet of the departure lounge while she was pulled away from him. At least she knew now that he loved her. Though, had she been given the choice, she'd have picked better circumstances than his mouthing the words as she was dragged away by armed government agents.

She had no idea if he was dead or alive. No one would tell her. Her only comfort was the fact that Doug was a trained soldier. He faced situations like this all the time, although she didn't want to think about the implications of that. He was strong. He knew what he was doing.

Worry for Doug had torn her heart apart, but she couldn't show even a hint of weakness to these people. They held the reins on her future, whether that meant a lifetime in jail or worse.

God, help me.

She looked at the agent across the table—a nameless, faceless suit and tie. The man studied her, as though trying to figure out why someone who had just bombed two different government facilities and killed at least a half-dozen people looked like she was about to cry.

"Ms. Laduca, I'm trying to help you. But I can't do that if you're not willing to give me anything."

"What's to give? The Raven is dead. I had nothing to do with her, except that she duped me for six years into running missions. All I did during that time was collect intelligence."

"Then explain this." The agent laid a picture of Christophe Parelli on the table between them.

Sabine sighed. "That wasn't me."

Her interrogator barked a laugh. "You're telling me you weren't there?" He laid down a surveillance photo of her in the hotel.

"I broke into the hotel suite. I got Parelli's hard drive. When Doug—Sergeant Major Richardson… When he interrupted me, someone else was already coming. Parelli and my mother came in behind us. We hid in the closet, and I saw her poison Parelli."

The agent tapped the table. His mouth worked back and forth. "Christophe Parelli was an informant for the U.S. government."

Sabine's stomach dropped. "I didn't know that."

"Evidently." The agent's jaw clenched. "What with you working for the Raven and all."

"I was duped."

"So you've said. And what kind of an agent does that make you, do you think? That you can't tell when the wool is being so completely pulled over your eyes."

Sabine swallowed. "Not a very good one."

She had thought her facade of a marriage to Maxwell was the end of it. She'd been so sure that she would never let herself be fooled again. But she had. Sabine had trusted someone and, like an idiot, had allowed herself to believe a lie. Again.

A shadow crossed over her heart. Was the love in Doug's eyes for real? Finally she'd found something— someone—who was worth believing in, and she found herself unable to let go.

Sabine felt arms wrap around her, despite the fact no one was near. It hit her deep inside, where she felt comfort at the thought of seeing Ben again. Where she knew Doug would be okay even if the worst had happened to him, God was reaching out to her.

With no movement or spoken word, Sabine reached back and found the solid foundation of a God who loved her without reservation. Not dependent on anything she had done. Love that defied explanation.

I believe, God. Help me trust You. No matter what happens.

Sabine felt like the tender new bud of a flower, fragile but with the deepest roots. Whatever happened to her, to Doug, she would be okay, because God was with her.

"Ms. Laduca, you're facing serious charges. Perhaps you should be more worried about what will happen to you."

More worried? She was clearly a better covert agent than she thought if he couldn't tell she was completely freaked out. Then again, perhaps this new warmth of peace in her chest had made its way to her face.

The agent collected up his papers. "I'll give you some time to think. But your options are pretty limited unless you can give us something that will sway us from putting you in jail for life." He stood. "It's up to you, Sabine."

The agent reached for the door handle.

"Wait."

He turned back. Sabine took a deep breath and pushed away the voices that said this was crazy. "I'll tell you everything I know. Everything I've done and learned over the last six years."

"You think that's good enough?"

"It's all I have."

The agent's eyebrows rose.

"Except—" Sabine lifted her chin. "Except…me."

The agent straightened. "I'm listening."

"What good is telling you what I know if you don't trust me?"

She was innocent. It could be argued that none of this was her fault, provided she ignored the fact that she should have known she was being duped. Should she even have to prove herself? Or was that just her pride telling her to be stubborn and refuse to start on the bottom rung of the ladder and earn her way back up?

It all boiled down to how badly she wanted to be an agent again. At one time it had been everything, her whole life. Just like Doug and the army. Then it had been about getting justice for Ben.

She had to know if she could trust herself, and right now that was seriously in doubt. She should ask them to put her in a teaching position, training new recruits. But could she mold new agents when she had failed so massively?

Could she do it? Could she earn back their trust? It was a crazy idea, but one that meant she would be free, at least to an extent. The CIA would have to be willing to work out a deal with her. One that meant she would go back to work for them, slowly working her way back to active status. She would never be the full agent she had once been. But she could still be an asset to them. Let them set whatever stipulations they wanted.

Because, if it meant she might get to see Doug, it didn't matter what the cost. *If he's still alive.*

The agent cocked his head to one side. "What is it you want, Agent Laduca?"

Sabine opened her mouth but couldn't say it. Going back into covert intelligence wouldn't make her happy. She was bone tired. What she really wanted was to walk away, to find a cottage on a beach somewhere and get started on the pile of books she'd bought but hadn't read yet.

"I want out."

The agent nodded. He walked back to the table and sat down. "This will be a long process, but I'm confident that with your cooperation we can work something out."

"Just like that, after threatening me with life in prison?"

"Make no mistake, Ms. Laduca, this won't be easy. You give us everything you know. And I mean every single thing you have from the last six years. Everywhere you went. Every person you talked to, every bug you planted and every computer file you stole. Then we'll talk about your being released. Completely under the radar, you live quiet as a mouse, and, if we ever call you…for anything, you do it. No questions."

"So I'm going to be your puppet forever?" Sabine shook her head. "Prison is starting to look appealing."

"The choice is entirely yours."

The constant pain left him breathless and, although he didn't want to admit it, very cranky. Between Jean and his father, Doug was never alone for a second. At that moment, Jean was straightening his blanket. He brushed her hands away and gave her a look.

The general was at the door, his arms folded.

Doug shook his head. "You look mad. What gives?"

"What gives?" The general stepped into the room. He walked carefully, and there were dark circles under his eyes, but Doug didn't think that was from the heart attack. "This isn't some joke, son. You've been hurt before, but never like this. You nearly died, and days later I find you putting your shoes on."

"You know why I have to find her, Dad. I'm going crazy not knowing where she is or what's happening."

She was in God's hands, but he was still going crazy not knowing.

The general sighed. "That's why I made some calls."

Doug's eyes widened. "And?"

"No one knows where she is. Colonel Hiller said they're refusing to even confirm that they have her."

"That's crazy. We all know she went with them. Where did they take her?"

"I'll find her, Doug, but I need time. And you need to rest up so you can get back to active duty."

He surged up from the bed. Pain lanced through his chest. "Sabine might not have time. I can't care about my job right now."

"Calm down." Tears filled his dad's eyes. "Please. You can't go get her if you're immobilized, and if you keep pushing it you're going to set yourself back. You're not invincible."

Doug forced himself to take slower breaths. He ducked his chin and immediately felt his dad's hand on the side of his neck.

"I don't want to lose you, too, son."

"I'm sorry."

"You have to trust me."

Doug nodded. He would trust his dad. They had never been this close, never in his whole life. All the strength he needed to lie back and let himself heal was there in his dad's touch.

Doug sucked in a lungful of air and blew out the need to dissolve into tears.

"Find her."

Eight days later Sabine was finally wrapping things up with the CIA when there was a knock on the door. She'd been in that same interrogation room from dawn until dinner every day and had lain awake nights in the glorified prison cell where her bed was. No contact with the outside world had left her bereft. She couldn't relax until she knew if Doug was okay.

The agent, the same one who'd interrogated her every day, glanced up. A familiar old man strode in wearing his dress army uniform with stars on his shoulders.

"Am I early?" His face split into a wide smile.

"Andrew," she whispered.

"My dear."

Sabine shot across the room and burrowed into his arms. She was taller than him, but it didn't matter. Doug's father folded her in his embrace. "How is he?"

The general nodded slowly, his eyes wet.

"How is he?" she repeated.

"He's worried about you, fighting everyone, refusing to listen to reason. Says he wants to leave the army."

"That's crazy. He loves being a soldier."

The general shrugged. "Says he's done. No one can get the why out of him. He's refusing to talk about it, demanding we find you. So I did. I can't have him rip out his stitches again, struggling and not listening to reason."

Sabine squeezed her eyes shut.

"Excuse me." The agent stood beside them. "Ms. Laduca is in our custody—"

"Not anymore."

Her face jerked back around and zeroed in on the general.

"You can't just waltz in here and yank this woman out—"

"I absolutely can, son." Andrew pulled out a trifolded paper and handed it to the agent. The agent studied it. His eyes widened. Andrew glanced at Sabine and winked.

She smiled back, reached up and touched his face. "Thank you."

He nodded.

The agent grunted. "This is highly irregular."

Sabine turned to him. "Our agreement stands. You know how to reach me."

She hooked her arm through the general's. She didn't care how it looked for a military officer to be outwardly affectionate. Apparently neither did he.

Out in the hall Andrew leaned in. "Agreement?"

Sabine shook her head. "A small price to pay for my freedom. If they decide to abuse the hold they have over me, I'll just disappear again." She ignored the look of worry in his eye. "Is Doug really leaving the army?"

"Seems so. We're all worried about him. It is so uncharacteristic to suddenly throw everything away."

Sabine sighed. "It's because of me, isn't it?"

He opened a door for her. "Would that be bad?"

"He loves being a soldier. It's everything to him."

Andrew's eyes darkened. "I don't think it's everything anymore."

"Are you sure?"

"Do you really have to ask that?"

"I know." She looked away as they walked. "He got shot protecting me. He nearly died, and now he's a mess. I can't help feeling guilty, like he would be better off if I had never come into his life. I can't help thinking that I failed at marriage before and I failed at my job now. I have nothing left, nothing to give him. And in return he's giving up everything he ever wanted."

She stopped and turned to his father. "I have to live a simple life now, and I'm okay with that. But how could Doug be happy with that? He needs action and a purpose. My life won't give him that. He'll be bored of me within a month."

The general's eyes were dark. "You sound like you're talking yourself into walking away."

Sabine hardened her heart against disappointing him. "I don't want Doug to be hurting. I can't stand hearing he's all worked up, worried about me and setting his recovery back." She waited for the affirmation. "He is, isn't he?"

"He's not doing himself any favors. How could he? He has no idea where his woman is. He's scared, Sabine."

"I was, too, not knowing if he was dead—" Her voice caught on the word.

Andrew touched her shoulders. "You love him."

Sabine nodded. She sniffed, wiped away a tear. "I'm not supposed to show emotion."

Andrew huffed. "Because bottling it up inside is so much better? You love my son. You tell him. Give him that, at least. When he's better, you see where things are at. Can you do that?"

She wasn't sure. It would mean being with Doug while he recovered, knowing she was going to walk away as soon as he was well again.

When she finally left this time, it would be so much harder for her. Doug could go back to his life physically recovered, and have the opportunity to be the career soldier he was meant to be. He might regret the loss of their relationship for a while, but eventually he'd find someone new.

Her heart tore open.

She shut her eyes. No more than a couple of weeks. Just long enough to make sure he was okay. In the meantime she would put her feelings aside and focus on helping him get better.

Sabine raised her eyes and looked at Andrew, hoping he didn't see the truth. "I can do that. I can give him time."

It didn't matter how much she loved him; he couldn't know. Not if it meant he was going to throw his life away.

NINETEEN

Andrew put the car in Park outside his home, and Sabine got out. Doug stepped carefully down the stone steps of the porch, his face lined with pain. She had hoped for more time to prepare before she saw him, time to get her thoughts and her heart on board with the plan. Too bad that wasn't going to happen.

She would be here for however long it took him to get back to full strength and see that the right decision for him was to stay with the army. It would take everything she had to keep her heart in one piece.

Doug stopped at the bottom step, and she didn't wait for him to come to her. Andrew passed by him and squeezed his shoulder, but Doug's eyes never left her. She remembered the way he'd shaken his head at her in the hospital, and this time she went straight into his arms. Sabine encircled his chest lightly, so as not to hurt him, and burrowed into him with her face in his neck.

"I love you."

Sabine burst into tears. She loved him, too, but she was going to walk away. There was no doubt in her mind that, despite the fact they loved each other, she wasn't the woman for him. The woman he married would support him, not get him shot and tear his life apart. It was better to cut the ties as soon as he was recovered, instead of getting in any deeper than she already was.

Sabine sucked in a breath. The CIA might have let her go, but it wouldn't be long before they considered her too much of a risk to be walking around. And there was no way she would let Doug get caught up in that.

She pulled away, wiped her cheeks and forced herself to let go of him. "You should be resting."

His eyes narrowed, but he didn't say anything about the distance she put between them. "Don't start. I have enough babysitters. I don't need one more."

"Too bad, because that's exactly what you've got." Sabine linked her arm with his and turned them to the door, but Doug held still.

She looked at him. "What is it?"

He studied her for a moment and then shook his head. "I was about to ask you the same thing."

"Doug—" She hated that she was playing this game. "I've had enough interrogation to last me the next ten years."

"So I'm not allowed to ask you anything?"

She let go of him. "I don't want to fight with you. That's not why I came here."

He looked at his sneakers for a moment and then back up at her. "I've been dreaming about this moment since I woke up in the hospital. I have to admit, I had a different picture of what our reunion was going to be like."

"Sorry I disappointed you."

"Are you really? I just told you that I loved you. Is there anything you'd like to say to me?"

Sabine swallowed. Apparently when she thought she could do this, she hadn't realized it would be the hardest thing she'd ever done in her life.

It's just another mission.

That didn't help. It was impossible to convince her heart not to break a little more every time she looked at him. They could never be together.

"I do love you."

It took everything she had to admit that out loud.

"Then why do you look so sad about it? What happened to you, Sabine? What did they do to you?"

He was right. Something had happened to her. Sitting in that interrogation room recounting everything she'd ever done as a spy, Sabine had realized that nothing about her was real.

For too long she'd played a part, never genuinely opening up and certainly not living life to the fullest. The missions she went on amounted to lying to get what she wanted. When she came home, there was little that was different. She'd lived a role with Maxwell, too, trying to be the perfect wife...at least until it all fell apart.

She kept herself removed from everything and everyone, got lost in books because it was a way to escape the pressure of trying to be...normal. Which was something she wanted more than anything else.

The only person who'd ever seen the truth was her brother, and he was gone. She hadn't thought it possible, but this man in front of her made her want to be real—to live.

God, give me the strength to do the right thing.

Doug touched her cheek, his hand sliding back into her hair. Sabine closed her eyes, felt the tickle on her cheek and realized she was crying again.

His lips touched one cheek and then the other, but the tears kept coming.

"Sabine—"

She shook her head. "Don't."

He kissed her—so softly—on the lips. "Tell me." His forehead touched hers. "Tell me."

She should have known he would never let her get away with it. Doug was the last person in the world she wanted to know how she really felt, the one person she wanted to guard herself from. He was the only person who could see the truth she hid behind her eyes.

She sucked in a breath. "Please don't make me do this."

She knew how he would feel when she walked away, because it was the same way she would feel—completely and utterly torn apart. They both needed to be strong.

Doug stepped back, and Sabine opened her eyes to the disappointment on his face. That hurt, too, but the only thing that was important was his recovery.

"I'll give you time. You can tell me when you're ready, but you will tell me."

She nodded.

Doug turned away and walked inside, taking her heart with him.

The movie credits rolled, and Doug looked over at Sabine, beside him on the couch. Lamplight illuminated the lines of her face, her closed eyes, the slow rise and fall of her breath as she slept. He stretched; the pain in his chest was a sharp ache but he didn't want a cloudy head from the medication.

Why was she was so hesitant to accept what was happening between them? What had the CIA told her? She was holding back everything, but why? Doug ached to make her tell him what the problem was, but she had to work it through in her mind before she could come back to him.

Her eyes flickered open. "I honestly thought you were dead, you know."

He sighed. "I'm sorry."

"Not half as sorry as I am. This was all my fault. If it wasn't for me, you'd never have been shot."

The look in her eyes broke his heart. "Like you could get rid of me that easily?"

She got up. Doug followed her into the kitchen. "Sabine—"

"Don't." She filled a kettle with water and set it on the stove. "It doesn't matter."

He laughed. She didn't mean that. Not when everything in her stance said she wanted to touch him, have him hold her again. "Because I'm not dead?"

"Yes."

Doug put his hands on her waist and turned her to him. "I'm sorry I joked about dying. You said you love me. You'll have to forgive me, because I'm going to be very happy about that."

"I said it doesn't matter."

"You can try to convince yourself of that all you want, Sabine, but it matters to me. It matters a lot."

"Why? There's no point. This can't go anywhere."

He knew she believed that, but he also didn't care anymore. "The fact that you think it can't go anywhere means you're acknowledging that there is something between us. I can work with that. All I have to do is convince you it'll be worth it."

Sabine didn't speak, so Doug gave her a small smile. "When you know what I see when I look at you, and what I feel when I touch you—" he took her hand "—then you'll be as convinced as I am that, while this might not be easy, it can be great. It doesn't matter how long it takes, Sabine. I've got all the time in the world to wait for you." He waited a beat. "What do you say?"

"I say okay."

His smile stretched. "Okay?"

She nodded. "I'm willing to let you convince me."

He leaned in to kiss her, but she sidestepped him and smiled. "Not like that."

"Why not?"

She dropped her hand, but he held it, not ready to let her go. She had the cutest look on her face, like she was trying hard to be serious.

"A kiss is not *convincing* me, it's swaying me to your way of thinking." She frowned. "When you kiss me I can't think straight. It's too easy to forget—why are you smiling?"

"Because I like hearing you say that." He squeezed her hand. "You make me happy. I like knowing I have an effect on you, too."

"There's a lot we have to work through, but I don't think there will ever be a lack of feeling between us."

"I'm glad to hear that, Sabine."

Doug settled for a kiss on her cheek. He didn't want to push her but still felt like he needed to stake a claim—a claim that would hopefully pay off with a relationship. The more time they spent getting to know each other, the stronger the foundation of their relationship would be later.

Her shoulders slumped and she frowned over the tea pot. When she yawned, his heart felt like it would burst. The woman was wrung out, physically and emotionally.

"Where'd your dad go?"

Doug leaned against the counter. "He took Jean to dinner. He wanted to give us some space—"

There was a short hum, and the power went out.

Sabine gasped. He reached out, found her shoulder and gave it a pat. "There's a flashlight in the cupboard beside the trash. Stay here, I'm going to go check the breaker."

Sabine found the flashlight where he said it would be and scanned the kitchen. The light illuminated a figure clad all in black, wearing a matching balaclava, who must have breached the general's security system. He was across the room by the back door. He looked like the same tall, wiry guy who'd been searching through Ben's room.

He raised a handgun and pointed it straight at her.

Of course the CIA would send someone to silence her. She just hadn't thought it would be this fast.

Before he fired, Sabine clicked off the flashlight and dropped to the floor. The gunshot illuminated the room around her. Surrounded by dark again, she crossed to the intruder. Retreat might be the gut reaction of the average civilian, but she had been trained to go toward danger instead of away from it—however unwise that might be.

She followed the sound of his footsteps and came up behind him. This needed to be finished before Doug came back from wherever the breaker switches were located.

She went for his head. An elbow flew back and connected with her temple. The pain was blinding, but she forced it away and kept a lock on the senses that told her where he was.

He slammed into her.

Sabine deflected blow after blow and managed to knock the gun to the floor, but this man was well trained and stronger than her. A brutal punch made her fall to her knees, and she fought away the instinct to panic. How had she ever managed to convince herself that dying was no big deal?

The intruder tackled her. Sabine shoved at him, but his hands grasped her neck and squeezed her throat shut. She groped for anything to use to defend herself…her fingers closed around the warm metal of the gun. She whipped it around and aimed dead center, but he knocked her arms away.

Then he was pulled off her.

Doug kicked and punched the man, his face bathed in rage.

Sabine grabbed his arm. "Stop!"

Doug froze.

"He's out cold."

The intruder was slumped at the bottom of the wall, unconscious.

"I'm okay." Sabine touched the sides of Doug's neck. His pulse was racing. "I'm okay."

Doug touched his forehead to hers and blew out a long breath. "This time we're calling the cops."

Sabine smiled.

"I'll give you some time." Colonel Hiller stood with his back to the railing, facing Doug. "You shouldn't rush into a decision like this. Retirement isn't easy. I've seen guys make that mistake. They wind up wasting time, and then they sign up again, but it's never the same."

Doug shifted on his seat and winced at the shard of pain but tried not to be obvious about it. He was saved when Sabine came out and laid a tray on the table with two steaming cups of coffee and a plate of cookies.

She didn't meet his eyes, just set it down and walked away.

Colonel Hiller said, "Are you sure this is what you want?"

Sabine hadn't spoken a word to him in the two days since he subdued the intruder in his dad's kitchen. That had been a fun conversation with the police. This whole thing was driving him crazy. Right when they were getting somewhere, some guy had broken in, and she had withdrawn into herself again.

Doug sighed. "Yes, I'm sure."

Was he?

Despite the distance she'd established between them, he was still certain she was the one for him. More certain than ever, even when he saw the conflict in her eyes. Beside him every minute, she was there to help with whatever he needed—except when what he needed was her. Then Sabine shuttered herself behind defenses he couldn't penetrate.

He could get past any obstacle he was faced with. Why not this? His training should count for something. Yet when he needed some hint of what she was feeling, she refused to give anything away.

Doug looked out over the lawns of his father's expansive yard. Doug had wanted to believe he could have his current way of life…and Sabine. The dream had to be possible, or else what had he been fighting for all these years? But something told him that his tenure with the army had come to an end.

What if God had a whole other plan for Doug?

TWENTY

He was going back to work.

Sabine tried to listen to the sermon, surrounded by a crowd of people all dressed in their Sunday clothes. Doug sat beside her, his focus on the open pages of his Bible. He glanced over at her, so she shot him a small smile and then looked back at the pastor. She would have trouble recounting what the man was talking about. Her Bible was flipped to the middle of Deuteronomy, but she couldn't focus.

She had to face the fact that Doug was going back to work. Soon he'd be flying off to his base in Texas, back to missions and a life that she wasn't meant to be a part of. It was time for Sabine to leave. She'd known it for three days now, since Colonel Hiller paid Doug a visit and she heard them talking.

Time to go. So why was she still here?

She had tried to guard her heart. It wasn't working. If she left now, it would hurt worse than ever, but eventually she would heal.

He leaned in and whispered in her ear. "Are you okay?"

She looked at him. Okay? Of course she wasn't okay. Doug wanted forever with her; he'd told her as much. Told her that he would wait until she sorted out…whatever it was that he thought was wrong with her.

Leaving was going to break both their hearts. She should just get it over with, like ripping off a Band-Aid, because being here was slow and painful torture. She saw it every time she looked in his eyes. He wanted to comfort her, to tell her every dream he was hiding in his heart.

Like the ones she hid in hers.

Sabine grabbed her purse and coat and stumbled to the aisle, past rows of congregants. People stared at her, but she ignored them and kept going. She pushed open the heavy double doors. The sky was low and gray and steady rain streamed down.

She trudged across the parking lot in the direction of Doug's truck and heard the sound of his shoes following behind her.

She turned…and squeezed her eyes shut. This was hard enough without seeing the pain of heartbreak in his eyes, too. "I have to go."

"I'll drive you. Wherever it is, we can go together."

Sabine shook her head. She felt his touch on her elbow. Her eyes flew open, and she stepped back. "I mean I have to *go*."

His eyes hardened. "Don't do this, Sabine. Don't walk out on us without even giving it a chance."

Sabine blinked against the sting of tears. She shouldn't have stayed for so long just because she couldn't find it in her to leave him. This was smart; it was the right thing. And it was going to be worse because she'd drawn it out.

"You were going to do this all along, weren't you? Ever since you showed up at the estate, this was your plan."

She winced as the roar built in his voice. "I—"

"Taking care of me but not really 'being' here. What was the point, if you weren't going to stick around?"

"Doug—"

"Don't lie to me. Tell me the truth. You were always going to walk away, weren't you?"

"Yes."

His face was damp. Rain soaked both of them, but she didn't know if he might be crying, too. "Why?"

"It's never going to work between us. I'm not the woman for you—"

"So you get to decide for both of us that this isn't going to work? I don't get a say at all?"

She shook her head. "It's not like that. This is for the best. You need to get on with your life without me…"

"Without you, what? Tell me why you're not the one when all I can think about is how right it feels having you here with me. Tell me. What?"

"You deserve better than me."

He blinked. "How can you say—"

"Because it's true." Sabine's world was crumbling, but she had to do this. "You need to be with someone who doesn't have a cloud of doubt over her head. I might have been officially cleared, but plenty of people still think I killed my team and betrayed this country. What would the army think if we got married? They'll be forever suspicious that you're feeding me information, or that I might turn you against this country."

She sniffed. "No one in charge is ever going to trust me. And if us being together means they won't trust you, either, then what's the point? I can't even ping on their radar or they'll haul me in for another round of interrogation—"

His eyes shut. "You should have told me."

"That you'll lose your job because you're too close to me? That everything you've worked for will be over because of me? Yeah, what a fun conversation that was going to be. So now you know. I won't be the one who ruins your life, okay? That's not what love is."

"God brought us together for a reason, Sabine."

"I know that. I believe that. I do. And it's been wonderful. I've never known anyone like you, Doug. But this is it. It has to be. God has someone for you, someone honorable who doesn't come with a classified past. Someone with a good life who comes from a good family. Someone who isn't me."

She turned away and ran. Her feet pounded the cement, splashed puddles and soaked the legs of her dress pants. *Never look back.* She ran until she couldn't run anymore, and then collapsed on a bus bench and sobbed.

Two days later Sabine parked the rental car she'd picked up at the airport in the driveway of a ranch-style house at the north end of Boise, where the oldest houses were. To get there she'd driven by the alley where the police had found her and Ben huddled behind the Dumpster all those years ago.

She looked out the windshield at a house shrouded in night and memories.

She steeled herself against the rush of the past and rummaged through her purse. The key had been among Ben's things. Why had she even chosen to come here? The place was probably full of spiders and woodland creatures trying to escape the wind and rain.

This was the only home she'd had until that horrible day she still couldn't seem to erase from her mind. A psychiatrist would probably have a field day with her inability to let go of the past. Or maybe it was normal that she'd never, ever forgotten, no matter how hard she tried. Who knew? She could only hope that being here now would somehow help her to make sense of the mess that was her life.

Inside the house she glanced around, her eyes wide. It looked the same. It hadn't degraded or deteriorated, nor was anything covered in dust. Someone had regularly cleaned the place…for years. Ben had done this. And he hadn't told her.

Sabine made her way to the kitchen. There she found a note on the table.

I don't know when, or even if, you'll read this, but here you are. I'm glad you came back. I'm proud of you for taking this step to get some closure on the past. I hope it helps you as much as it helped me. I love you, big sister.
Ben

Her sobs echoed around the place where she had once had a family, while she grieved for the family she could have had with Doug—the family of her heart.

Doug sat at the kitchen table in his father's house with the newspaper and stared at the black ink, not seeing any of the words.

"This is ridiculous, son."

Doug sighed. He knew the picture he made wasn't pretty. The week's growth of beard itched, and his eyes were probably bloodshot. His sweatpants and T-shirt were sort of clean.

"I didn't get that girl out of CIA custody for you to let her walk away."

"She wanted to go." Doug rubbed a hand down his face. "It was her idea."

His dad pulled out a chair and sat. "You think I don't know that? You think I didn't know she came here with every intention of hiding exactly what she felt for you and how much she loves you?"

"You're wrong."

"That she loves you? I don't think so. Your mother did the same thing, son. Told me there was no way that a diner waitress who lived in a trailer and hadn't even graduated high school was going to marry an officer. Said I should forget about her and get on with my life."

Doug rolled his eyes. "Mom was not a diner waitress."

"She was when I met her."

"You said you guys met in a restaurant."

Andrew smiled and shrugged. "Thereabouts."

Doug looked up. "Why are you telling me this now, anyway? What's the point of this pep talk?"

His dad leaned closer. "Because you apparently need me to explain something to you that any fool can see. That girl loves you so much it scares her, because she's watching her life fall apart and looking to you for safety, only to find you throwing away yours."

"I'm not going back to the army."

"Since when?"

"Since her. There's something out there for us to do together, something better."

"You never explained that to her. You just let her walk away because it wasn't going the way you thought it was supposed to go." His dad paused. "I made that mistake, too, and I almost lost the best thing that ever happened to me. Until I realized I'd give it all up to have your mother, even the army."

"But you didn't. I did."

"Very nearly did, son. Had the papers and everything. Your mother hit the roof." His dad chuckled. "Finally she said she'd marry me just so I didn't throw my life away."

Doug frowned at him. "Mom married you so you wouldn't leave the army?"

"That's exactly right." He patted Doug's shoulder. "Maybe leaving to go be with your woman is right for you, son. If that's what you did, I'm certain when you tell her, she'll make sure you never regret it for one minute of the rest of your life. That's the kind of woman she is."

"I don't want her indebted to me."

"Tell her that." His dad drew a small velvet box from his pocket and laid it on the table between them. "And give her this. It's what your mother would have wanted."

TWENTY-ONE

One month later
Barcelona, Spain

"Bye. Thank you. See you all tomorrow!"

Sabine received hugs and kisses from each of the children and ushered them out of her classroom to where their mothers waited. They were all adorable and so eager to learn English that it made her job easier than anything she'd ever done.

Her Spanish had been a little rusty at first. Within days of being saturated with the Spanish culture and such a beautiful language, she had rediscovered the nuances of it.

Blanca entered the back of the classroom. In a matter of weeks the older woman had become so dear to Sabine—something that had surprised her. After all, she'd never had a healthy relationship with an older woman in her whole life.

Together they cleaned up the school supplies, and Sabine swept the floor. When Blanca didn't set down the dust pan for her, Sabine looked up. "What is it?"

"You know you can tell me anything, child." Blanca's eyes were bright, even surrounded by fine lines. The strands of silver in her dark hair made her more beautiful, and Sabine could tell that as a young woman Blanca had been breathtakingly gorgeous.

"I know. It's just—"

The old woman nodded slowly. "Heartbreak is not an easy thing to heal."

"How did you know?"

"The Good Lord, He tells me things."

Sabine hadn't told any of the staff at the school. Or anyone she had met at the small church up the hill that had been started by missionaries. It was an outreach to the local children, kids from poor families who came to school in ill-fitting clothes and worn sandals. None of them knew where she came from, or why she'd just shown up one day, willing to help out. They'd given up asking.

Apparently they didn't need to ask.

Sabine smiled. "Did He tell you anything else?"

The old woman's mouth curled up, and her eyes sparkled. "I'll finish tidying up. Why don't you take a walk along the cliff top? I've seen you eyeing that book reader thing sticking out of your purse."

The e-reader had been a gift Sabine had bought to console herself. Aside from the time she spent teaching, she was practically attached to the thing. She gave Blanca a kiss on the cheek and surprise lit up the old woman's face.

Sabine walked the path along the cliff that overlooked the ocean. The sun permeated everything until it was impossible to believe it was anything but a beautiful summer anywhere in the world. It just seemed as if, since it was so nice here, it should be this nice everywhere.

Ocean breezes fluttered the skirt of her knee-length flowery summer dress as she walked. When she reached the bench, she sat carefully so the splintered wood didn't catch on the fabric and pulled out her e-reader.

A seagull swooped a wide arc that drew her eyes from

the screen. She watched it twist and rise, much like the journey Sabine's heart had taken the past few months. Rising from the depths of grief, she had found peace and hope in Jesus. His love filled her to overflowing, washing over her like the waves on the shore.

Everything seemed so right. She had what she wanted—freedom, peace and the chance to live the life she had always dreamed of.

So why did it feel like there was still something...missing?

Footsteps ascended the path up the cliff, the gait heavy. Sabine turned. The old instinct to flee pulled her to her feet. She skirted the bench and backed away.

He stopped and frowned. "Come here, Sabine." It was the first word of English she'd heard outside of her classroom in a month, and it sounded beautiful. His khaki slacks and light blue button-down shirt made him look like a businessman on vacation. A very good-looking businessman who seemed interested in a holiday romance.

Tears blurred her vision. "Why did you come?"

"You mean why have I been searching the whole world for the last month? Or why did I leave the army? Because the answer to both is the same. You."

"I— You can't just—"

He closed the gap between them. "I did."

She shook her head and stepped back. "I won't go through this again. There's no point in rehashing all of this just because you came here. You shouldn't have... You need to go."

She brushed past him and fled down the hillside. Not a hundred yards from the bench, he caught up to her.

"Stop running away from me."

She turned back. "Nothing has changed. I don't know why you came, or why you want to bring it all back up again. Are you trying to hurt me on purpose? Is that it? You want to get back at me."

"I would never do that to you, Sabine."

She ignored the way his eyes softened, the light touch of his fingers on her elbow. "Why did you come here? What's different now? There's still no way we can be together, so why are you prolonging it? It hurts too much, Doug. I'm trying to heal. I'm trying to get on with my life."

Doug touched her cheek. There were tears in his eyes now. "I won't let you go again. You're only seeing the obstacles and letting what you assume I want cloud your judgment. Don't you think that I want to be with you? I mean, seriously…I could get a job as a plumber, and I'd not only be happy, but I'd get down on my knees every single day and thank God that you believed in us enough to let me love you. That you believed in what we could be together enough to love me."

"Those are nice words, Doug. But I can't imagine that you'd be happy without dangerous missions to go on, plus the greater good and the impact your job has on the world." She bit her lip and shook her head. "That's a huge part of who you are, and now it's just gone? How can you be okay with that?"

"How are *you* okay with it? Rogue or not, you had missions, and you believed the work you did was important. Was it just a job, or was it something more?"

"It was everything."

His eyes were soft. "And now that you've lost it all?"

She looked out over the valley. "I don't need a mission. But since I've been here, I've loved teaching these kids. To know I'm making a difference with just one of them… It feels good."

"Because you want to do something that matters."

She nodded.

"Do you want some help?" He shrugged, and a smile curled the corners of his mouth. "I like kids. What if we did something together, like an outreach or a drop-in center? Fostering. Mentoring. There's a whole world of options, Sabine. We could do anything."

Sabine took a deep breath.

He frowned. "Do you believe in us enough for that?"

"I'm scared. I love you so much, but what if it isn't enough?"

He reached up and wiped the tears from her cheeks. "Just promise me one thing. Promise me you'll always fight for us. That you'll take all that passion and strength you have in you and put it into building something with me."

He really saw her that way? Sabine's heart swelled until she thought it would burst from her chest. "I promise. I'm sorry I ran away."

He touched his forehead to hers. "I'm sorry I let you go."

Sabine opened her mouth. He covered it with his fingers. "The time for talking is over."

Doug drew her into his arms. His mouth covered hers, and he kissed her in a way she'd never been kissed before. It was full of passion and the promise of a rich life. She smiled against his lips as the sun wrapped them in a cocoon of warmth.

From a distance, someone clapped. It turned into more people clapping, and then someone cheered. When Doug released her, she glanced around, dazed to find the entire staff on the hillside watching them.

She looked back at Doug.

"I love you. Do you love me?" There was so much worry written on his face. Was he wondering if he had made a mistake?

"How can you even ask me that?"

He stayed still. "Is that a yes?"

She nodded. "Of course I love you."

"Then you'll marry me?"

"Where will we live? What will you do?"

He rolled his eyes, but there was a smile there. "Can you just answer the question, please?"

"Yes, of course I will, but—"

He cut her off again, his fingers on her lips. "We'll figure it out, honey. But honestly, so long as we're together, I don't really care."

"Oh." She smiled. "That's a good answer."

He pulled her to him again and wrapped his arms around her. Sabine buried her face in his neck. She laughed and felt his chest shake with his own laughter.

At long last she had found a place to belong. She'd thought it would be a home or a family to love her, and she would have those things now, too. But at the center of it all, she had a Father in Heaven who loved her and had blessed her life beyond what she thought possible.

Because He'd given her Doug.

* * * * *

Dear Reader,

Thank you for going on this journey with Doug and Sabine, my first book for the Love Inspired Suspense line. I hope it was as fun to read as it was for me to write!

In *Double Agent,* Doug and Sabine are both confined by the chains of their pasts, until they surrender their lives to the Lord. The shame and guilt we suffer because of the things we've done, or the decisions we've made, can stay with us. But God is truly the only one who can bring freedom in our lives. His love can break those chains.

To find out more about me and my books you can go to www.authorlisaphillips.com or you can email me at lisaphillipsbks@gmail.com. If you're not online, you can write to me c/o Love Inspired Books, 233 Broadway, Suite 1001, New York, NY 10279. I would love to hear from you.

God bless you richly,
Lisa Phillips

Questions for Discussion

1. Doug and Sabine both want to find Ben's killer, so they team up. Why do you think Doug agreed to this? What would you have done?

2. What do you think made Sabine want to be a spy? Do you think it would be an exciting job or a scary one? Why?

3. Both Doug and Sabine discover things about each other they never knew. Do you know people who have a different persona they adopt in different situations? How do you feel about this?

4. Do you think part of Sabine's "spy" persona had to do with self-preservation? Have you ever done something similar? Why?

5. Doug and Sabine make up a mixed-race couple. How do you feel about love that crosses the boundaries of race and culture?

6. Both Doug and Sabine have the kind of job where only those closest to them know. Have you ever had a secret? What happened?

7. Sabine admits her brother reacted badly when he found out she was a spy. Have you had good or bad reactions to your secrets? Why do you think that is?

8. Doug assumes—incorrectly—that Sabine uses her feminine wiles to charm her targets. Has anyone ever

drawn a wrong conclusion about you? Why? How did it make you feel?

9. Doug and his father have a complex relationship, to where he feels he can't even tell him he misses him. Why do you think this is?

10. Doug feels as if his mother was the one who brought him and his father together. Is there someone in your life or your family who holds people together? Why do you think this is?

11. The middle-aged housekeeper, Jean, clearly feels protective of Doug's father, and the general has kept her in his employ for years. Do you feel they could have a romantic relationship? What do you think it would take for them to fall in love, or even admit how they feel?

12. Sabine wakes up at her house to find Doug has both gone grocery shopping and made breakfast. How do you feel about a man who will take care of a woman this way?

13. Sabine believes she's not worthy of a relationship where she is loved and treasured. Have you ever felt like this? Why? What, if anything, made you change your mind?

14. Sabine keeps from Doug the fact her handler is the same man he knew, a major general, not wanting to sully his reputation now that he is dead. Do you agree with her wanting to protect Doug's memories? Or do you think the truth should always come out?

15. After finding out her handler's identity, Sabine intends to go and resolve the situation herself—without the team's help. Do you think she could have done this? Have you ever taken something on like this? Why?

REQUEST YOUR FREE BOOKS!

2 FREE RIVETING INSPIRATIONAL NOVELS
PLUS 2 FREE MYSTERY GIFTS

Love Inspired®
SUSPENSE

The marshals are closing in on the illegal adoption ring, and Serena and her partner Josh must team up to bring it down for good.

*Read on for a preview of the exciting conclusion to the **WITNESS PROTECTION** series, UNDERCOVER MARRIAGE by Terri Reed, from Love Inspired Suspense.*

U.S. marshal Serena Summers entered three-year-old Brandon McIntyre's room with a packing box in hand. Her heart ached for the turmoil the McIntyre family had recently suffered. Danger had touched their lives in the most horrible of ways. A child kidnapped.

But thankfully rescued by the joint efforts of loving parents and the marshal service.

The McIntyre family no longer lived in Houston. The U.S. marshal service had moved them for a second time when their location had been compromised.

Only a few people within the service knew where Dylan, Grace and the kids had been relocated.

Serena and her partner, Josh, were among them. It was their job to pack up the family's belongings and forward them through a long and winding path to their final destination.

Serena's fingers curled with anger around a tiny tennis shoe in her hand.

So many deaths, so many lives thrown into chaos.

The thought that someone she had worked with, trusted, had stolen the evidence and had been leaking information to the bad guys sent Serena's blood to boil.

If her brother were alive, he'd know how to compartmentalize the anger and pain gnawing at her day in and day out.

But Daniel was gone. Murdered.

A sharp stab of grief sliced through her heart. Followed closely by the anger that always chased her sorrow.

"Hey, you okay in here?"

Serena glanced up at her current partner, U.S. marshal Josh McCall. He'd taken off his navy suit jacket and rolled the sleeves of his once crisp white dress shirt up to the elbows. His brown hair looked like he'd been running his fingers through it again, the ends standing up. She'd always found him appealing. But that was before. Now she refused to allow her reaction to show. Not only did she not want to draw attention to the fact that she'd noticed anything about him, she didn't want him to think she cared.

She didn't. Josh was the reason her brother had been alone when he'd been murdered.

Turning away from Josh, she said briskly, "I'm good."

Taking the two ends of the sheet in each hand, she spread her arms wide and attempted to fold the sheet in half.

"Here," Josh said, stepping all the way into the room. "Let me help."

He reached for the sheet, his hands brushing hers.

An electric current shot through her. She jerked away, letting go of the ends like she'd been burned. "I don't need your help."

His hand dropped to his side. "Serena." Josh's tone held a note of hurt.

Glass shattered.

Someone else was in the house.

Pick up UNDERCOVER MARRIAGE by Terri Reed, available June 2014 from Love Inspired® Suspense.

Love Inspired
SUSPENSE
RIVETING INSPIRATIONAL ROMANCE

Hometown secrets

Was the explosion that took the lives of Sarah Russell's parents an act of murder? Her teenaged daughter thinks so and is determined to seek answers in their sleepy small town. Sarah fears her daughter will uncover a secret she's not ready to share: everyone—including Sarah's daughter—believes the girl is Sarah's kid *sister*. Even the child's father doesn't know the truth. But as Sarah reunites with Nick Tyler to look into the mysterious deaths, she knows she'll have to tell him—and her daughter—the truth. Yet someone wants to ensure that no one uncovers *any* long buried secrets.

COLLATERAL DAMAGE
by
HANNAH ALEXANDER

Available June 2014 wherever
Love Inspired books and ebooks are sold.

LIS44599